flight 404

simon petrie

This edition first published in Australia in 2018

Please direct all enquiries to the publisher at:
fomalhaut451@gmail.com

ISBN 978-0-6483228-4-9

Typeset in Adobe Garamond Pro / Candara
Cover artwork by Lewis P Morley
Cover and internal design by Simon Petrie

National Library of Australia Cataloguing-in-Publication entry

Title:	Flight 404 / Simon Petrie.
ISBN:	9780648322849 (pbk.)
Subjects:	Science fiction, Australian.
Other Authors / Contributors:	
	Harvey, Edwina, editor.
Dewey Number:	A823.4

flight 404

simon petrie

books by simon petrie

(the titan sequence)

Matters Arising from the Identification of the Body

Wide Brown Land

A Reappraisal of the Circumstances Resulting in Death (forthcoming)

Flight 404

Murder on the Zenith Express: the Gordon Mamon collection

80,000 Totally Secure Passwords That No Hacker Would Ever Guess

For Hamish and Elizabeth

one

'They're dead. They're all dead.'

The comment, innocent of deeper intent, is on the flowers withering in a glass vase. But there's a flash of panic, in response, that I only perceive on later re-examination.

It starts as a simple vessel-delivery run, Sol to Eps Eri. Just a mission, though there are undercurrents from the start. I thought I'd turned my back on Eps Eri, and on my birth planet, Ashé, for good, two decades ago. But nothing lasts forever.

Still, Ashé cannot retain a traction over me. (Or so I tell myself. Big girl now.)

Around Eps Eri, the interplanetary search for the vanished deep-space passenger vessel *Bougainvillaea* is well in train; *Peregrinator*, my command for the next few hours, is late to the party. Late, and slicing so much faster than light through the cloth that is the Universe's most-mysterious fabric. To the Galaxy around me, I am temporarily no more than a concept, my ship no more than a potentiality, distance itself only the merest suggestion. It's an unnerving, ill-grasped proposition, not dispelled by the perceived solidity of my seat-strapped body, the ship's command station, the vessel itself. I know that there are people for whom altspace travel is something exciting and tinged with glamour. I do not understand such people.

Peregrinator is – or will again be, when we revert to urspace – a decommissioned corvette, Reaver class, newly refitted as a dedicated, single-occupant search-and-reconnaissance craft. Fast, manoeuvrable, crammed with sophisticated sensors and tech-toys that the Borken corporation has been itching, these past few months, to give a tryout. (Be careful what you wish for…)

I'd be curious enough, myself, to see how *Peregrinator* performs. Instead, it's Wlodek who gets the hot seat on this one. (Anders Wlodek, longtime Borken employee, local rep, edging retirement, former pilot. *Former* pilot.)

My instructions: get to Utgard. Handover. Wait out the days, weeks, maybe months there, until the DSSAR mission has run its course. Easy pay. But the habitats and colonies that comprise Utgard, scattered in orbit around Eps Eri's gas giant Jotunheim, are no place to get stuck for an extended stretch. Moreover, I don't see where in the equation "former pilot" gets to confer any advantage over "pilot". Particularly since, though I know little of Wlodek's history, he cannot be that high an achiever to have wound up at an outpost like Ashé. And in any case *Peregrinator* has sufficient smarts for a mission of this type, regardless of who's playing "meat culprit" at the helm. A personnel switch doesn't make sense: with the hours lost in handover, Borken's state-of-the-art assets will get to the search zone later. Not my business, but it rankles.

It remains to be seen, in any case, whether there will be anything to find. The search is into its tenth daycycle, a dozen ships scouring the region of the *Bougainvillaea*'s disappearance: no trace.

Doesn't look good. I don't envy anyone waiting for news on the fate of their loved ones. Nor anyone explaining to those waiting why Borken might have chosen to delay its arrival on the scene of what is potentially the corporation's worst spaceflight incident. (Borken HQ, I gather, would have preferred to leave things to local authorities. But, keen to protect its local reputation, Borken's Eps Eri subsidiary has pushed for involvement from Central.)

Not my business. But it rankles. *Former* pilot.

We emerge from altspace. As part of that transaction, eight point five nine seven pristine kilograms of indium-113 vanishes, its purpose met, its fate unknown. As another part of that transaction, I resist the urge to vomit (because it never helps). When the scraped-raw pain and throb of the reality shift recedes, I take in the comforting view of *Peregrinator*'s messy command station around me – have to do some station-keeping before we rendezvous with Wlodek – and check our situation.

Not good. Not by a long way. *Peregrinator* is approximately fifty million km out from Ashé, over two hundred million km from the last reported location of the *Bougainvillaea*, and almost three hundred million inwards of Jotunheim. There's always a degree of hit-and-miss to altflight nav, but *this* is disastrous. It makes no sense at all, now, to proceed as per my instructions, to handover to Wlodek…

Peregrinator's mission has scarcely begun, and already it's in turmoil.

Most systems, we should be clear to proceed directly to the search area.

Eps Eri isn't most systems.

The appropriate documentation has been hastily filled out. K@rine, my wood-skinned android, sends the proxy on its way. It won't, of course, suffice to legitimise our presence here. An accompanying courtesy call to Ashé TransMig, perhaps? (Though bureaucrats, anywhere, ask a lot of questions, and the five-minute transmission turnaround is a hassle. Not my speed: I'll settle for other approaches, *danke*.)

Peregrinator sees to her own navigation – which means "not running into anything" in Eps Eri's rubbish-wracked IPM, as much as it does setting a course which can be tailored either for flight to Ashé, or to the search area. The captain's chair has, under sustained high-*g* boost, induced a crimping pain around my lower spine and kidneys. I rise, and climb carefully "down" to my quarters. Submitting to the automated embrace of the acceleration couch (or "splatter guard" as I prefer to think of it), I heads-up the couch's auxiliary command feature, instruct *Peregrinator* to pile on another half-*g* accel. Then I compose a bare-bones text transmission, informing Wlodek of my command decision. Curiously, the closing platitude is the most difficult part of the message; I send it, before I allow myself too many second thoughts.

Wlodek won't be happy.

Space is wide. There's a lot of empty time, in a transit...

... and K@rine is, once again, extrapolating from my memories.

'What I don't get,' "Miguel" is saying, 'is why you didn't go for Rio at the same time.'

4

'One, I didn't *want* reorientation, still don't; and two, it really is none of your fucking business. So to speak.'

'But you could have fitted right back into society,' "Miguel" argues. 'It would have made things so much more straightforward for you. And nobody would have been any the wiser.'

I sigh. 'Fitted back into society, Mig? Yours, perhaps. Not mine.'

'Yours too, I thought.' There is, somehow, a suggestion of disappointment in the woodgrained face's unchanging expression. K@rine is getting disconcertingly accomplished in these nuances. The advocate for all my devils.

'I would've been destroying myself... look, that's overbitten, maybe, but at least denying myself. And I'd done enough of that already.'

'Why didn't you explain any of this stuff at the time?' "Miguel" asks.

'How could I? Look, you know what Ashé was like. *Is* like, as far as I can tell. I left because Ashé was never going to be comfortable with what I was, and I was never going to accept its version of what I was supposed to be. Who I was supposed to be. Who I *am*.'

'But you *were*—'

'No. No, Mig, I wasn't. And I'm sorry if that ruins all your memories of what we had growing up, but frankly that's your problem not mine. I was never right, never *at home*, in that body. It might have seemed that way to you, but it wasn't. It was a million *years* from right.'

'You could've made it right.' "Miguel" has something in his tone – not quite accusation, not quite petulance – that sends a shiver.

'Only by conforming to Ashé's ridiculously hidebound ideals of alignment. Mig, I had an absolutely *miserable* boyhood, for the most part. No offence. Drawing a line under it, taking a knife to it, was the best thing I ever did.'

'But—'

'Look, can we stop now?' I ask.

Something indefinable vanishes from K@rine's mahogany visage as it drops the pretense. 'Was that... accurate?' it asks. Always, the first concern of the machine.

'Accurate? K@rine, how should I know? I haven't seen Miguel for eighteen years.'

'Yet you still speak of him, on occasion.'

'He was part of my youth, part of what shaped me. But it would be like – I don't know, like if you were to talk about one of your developers.'

'I didn't have developers, Charmain.' Is the machine *chiding* me? Its wooden mask presents no clue.

'My point is... if there was someone from your past, your origins, who you spoke about from time to time, your description wouldn't be exactly accurate.'

'My memories—'

'People *change*, K@rine. So it's pointless to pretend, just because I knew someone two decades ago, that I still know them now.'

'Are you saying you didn't find the simulation helpful?'

'No. No, K@rine, I'm not saying that.'

I've no real appetite, in these surroundings, for revisiting the past. But I get the feeling K@rine is going to persist.

*

Like most planets, Ashé has a beauty about it, a fractal grandeur, when seen from sufficient distance to gloss over the messy human detail of settlements; orbitals; factories. I'm not about to spoil the illusion through heightening the magnification.

We're playing a risk. I've kept *Peregrinator* under steady boost: a stopover at Ashé would slow us unacceptably. But at the speed we're currently making, we'll be spending less than an hour within a moon's-orbit radius of the planet. An hour may not be enough to secure the TransMig clearance we need.

The grey-brown-blue swirl of the planet's equatorial skin is replaced by a ruddy visage, shaven, lined, serious. Grey-white hair, cut crew, nose rather fleshy for so slender a face. Not, I think, a face which smiles often, or in company.

I've seen that jawline before, elsewhere. My chest tightens.

'Ms Mertz.'

Even on those two nondescript syllables, the voice sounds as I've expected. Ashé is a less-than-free player in intersystem politics and trade, and this self-imposed isolationism has yielded a distinctive and at times self-parodying planetary accent. In its way, it's seductive in its lilting familiarity. But two decades of Galactic normalisation of my own dialect is not so easy to shake free, even had I wished. Which I do not: letting my accent go native, here, now, with this official, could take things along any of a half-dozen different vectors, none of them fruitful.

'Greetings. But call me Charmain, please,' I offer, knowing full well he won't. With a squint, I feign difficulty in reading the official's badge, though the surname, at least, is one I already know. 'Officer Jurgen… Demetriades?'

There is a three-second lightspeed delay, during which a jolt arrives. It's one of dozens of small impacts, a featherweight dustsplat onto *Peregrinator*'s armour-thick nosecone. The dust-blows have become commonplace enough that I've been mentally filtering them, just a feature of traversing local space in Eps Eri's dust-filled environs. On this occasion, in all probability, I mark it only because I'm listening.

'*Demetriodes*,' he corrects, overplaying the syllables as one does for a foreigner. 'To what do we owe this... incursion?'

'Incursion?'

'Ms Mertz. Your vessel is Sol-registered. You are transgressing Epsilon Eridani's interplanetary medium, without Ashé permission, let, or authority.'

'My apologies, Officer Demetriodes. I had hoped my proxy might have explained this already. I *did* send you a proxy, didn't I?'

The visual feed chops, momentarily, then recovers. 'You sent seven, Ms Mertz. Of quite impressively progressing sophistication. None of which, however, managed to adequately account for the incursion of your *Peregrinator* – a military-capable craft, under the command of a Sol-registered individual. We already have a full complement of military and rescue crews active within the search zone. Why is a Sol-registered vessel such as yours so concerned to join the search for a Tau Ceti-registered ship, reported in Epsilon Eridani's space? You have no jurisdiction here. And it smacks of typical Sol arrogance to presume, as you apparently do, that you and your craft can somehow succeed in finding what our own resources have yet to uncover.'

'On the subject of "Sol arrogance",' I reply, bristling, 'we are merely doing local bidding. *Peregrinator* is here on request of Borken's Eps Eri-based operations, headed by Anders Wlodek, a naturalised Ashéan citizen.'

'Then where is—'

He says more during the delay, but I don't bother to listen before I reply. 'Wlodek's at Utgard,' I explain, allowing a weariness into my tone. 'Which was the original destination of our altspace trajectory. Believe me, passage through Ashéan local space was never our intention,' I say, talking at sufficient volume that he cannot help but overhear even if he is himself still speaking. 'We are just here for the *Bougainvillaea*'s flight data recorders, Officer Demetriodes. Once Borken's technical experts have reviewed the circumstances of the incident, we will, of course, provide Ashé's authorities with copies of all data we obtain, in accordance with accepted inter-system treaties.'

'To which Ashé itself is not a signatory,' he reminds me, after a four-second pause. 'More to the point, we were given to understand that your craft would be commanded by an Anders Wlodek, who you now tell me is not even on board your vessel. While I concede that you do indeed identify as a representative of Borken Corporate, you lack TransMig accreditation. You can be assured Borken's local subsidiary will be informed in due course, if our rescue crews discover anything of relevance—'

'Not good enough,' I interrupt. Or *think* I interrupt.

'—but I am not disposed to accede to your req—' And now, only now, my interjection has arrived. Demetriodes' frown deepens, and his slow exhale is audible. When he resumes, it's in a lower register, and slower. '*Not disposed* to accede to your request. Please stand down your ingress of Ashé's sovereign territory.'

'As you wish, of course. But what of the salvage craft?'

'Salvage craft?'

'Our intelligence suggests the local presence of three Tau-Ceti-registered vessels which we believe to have interdicted Eps Eri territory, in the wake of the *Bougainvillaea*'s status report. Tell me, is it still TransMig policy to summarily reject all requests for in-system access by intersystem vessels, except on clearly-delineated passenger and freight missions?'

'I am not aware,' he replies carefully, 'of these Tau Ceti salvage craft to which you refer.'

'Perhaps so.' I take a breath, and hope that our intelligence as to the salvage vessels' identities is reliable. 'But the presence of salvors such as, say, the *Slithy Tove*, the *Kokopelli*, for argument's sake, and the *Now Just Cut That Out* would suggest a failure of TransMig oversight. In one form or another.'

Closest approach. Transmission delay is now down to a mere two seconds. Soon, inevitably, it will begin to climb.

'Ms Mertz,' Demetriodes replies, after a twenty-second pause. 'What do you mean, *failure of oversight*?'

'Merely that the salvage rights on a vessel as large as the *Bougainvillaea*, assuming that worst has come to worst, would be on the high end of phenomenal. One might imagine that, for Ashé to forgo such rights to out-system vessels, a hefty one-time license fee might well have been levied on the salvage craft.'

'I assure you that—'

'In which case, the suggestion that an Ashé bureaucratic department might have contravened TransMig restrictions in exchange for substantial out-system credit payments would have to, I think, be a matter of considerable interest to your own watchdog groups and probity overseers.'

'Ms Mertz—'

'Officer Demetriodes. Our Sol-system documentation is *bona fide*. We have genuine cause for haste, in attempting to obtain our own copy of the flight data where the primary evidence might well be obtained by vessels which are unlikely to remain in the vicinity for any longer than they deem necessary, or potentially profitable. Your concern for the safety and security of Eps Eri's interplanetary medium is admirable, but it is through a drive to enhance flight safety that we ourselves are here now. We've come a long way, Officer Demetriodes. We seek only what's rightfully ours, a statement which may not be true of certain out-system salvage vessels. We need only TransMig authorisation to allow us to proceed. Our mission is peaceful and of some importance. Please don't let it have been in vain.'

'Regulations require that all applications for in-system access must be presented in person—'

'Did the crew of the *Slithy Tove* make application in person?' I ask. 'Or the others?'

'I cannot divulge those details.' Meaning he very probably doesn't know. A frown crosses his face.

I press my advantage. 'It would be a pity,' I begin, 'if Borken was prevented from reaching the search zone, in the circumstance that an out-of-system salvage vessel were to find the *Bougainvillaea*'s wreckage. Particularly if said salvage vessel were found to have connections to one of Borken's competitors. The proceedings from such a situation would necessarily be bitter, protracted, and litigious, and would embroil Ashé, or more to the point TransMig, in a considerable degree of unpleasant and in all likelihood expensive attention. Central to this attention, of course, would be any TransMig officials who had directly and actively opposed Borken's access.'

The frown deepens, and his face settles into an expression of impotent hostility before, eventually, he speaks. 'Please state the duration of your intended transit of Ashé's sovereign territory.'

Not before time.

Onscreen, the sun is rising over the eastern seaboard of Penitence, the broad desert-raddled continent that smears almost eighty percent of the way around Ashé's equator. I imagine families, in the various arcologies, cooberpedies, and steel-shuttered towns of my home prefecture, rising in readiness to meet the day's challenges, offering prayer, meditation, and ritual to the divine agency of their choice as they break the long night's fast. (They're fond of saying, on Ashé, that it matters less *what* you believe than that your belief is strong. It's not true, of course – a week in any outlying settlement will convince you otherwise – but they're fond of saying it. Because they *want* to believe it.)

There's a satisfaction in having so plainly played Demetriodes, in having accordingly sidestepped Wlodek, which lasts for several minutes; until K@rine reveals what it has found among the Bougainvillaea's official passenger manifest.

Things turn icy pretty quick. And plans change.

two

Two dancers, Shock and Disbelief, move to the tune of a slow, cold waltz. On a bench at the edge of the cavernous hall, I sit, numb, watching, while Guilt sidles up towards me, lays its sweat-warm hand upon my knee.

I had not made any kind of communication to my sister for several years. The inconvenience and expense of altspace transmission makes for a useful excuse; but it *is* just an excuse, and not enough.

There's so much I had not known. I hadn't even known that Nasreen had moved further out, from the Tau Ceti habitats to the new terraforming project at HD 4391. (And I thought *I'd* put a lot of distance between Ashé and myself.) I hadn't known she'd re-partnered, had never met this Jian; and while I'd been aware, somewhere, that Ahmed was no longer an infant, eight would not have been the age I'd have picked. It went to show.

I didn't have the faintest notion what her name, her new partner's name, her son's name, were doing on the passenger list for the *Bougainvillaea*. Perhaps a once-in-a-decade vacation, perhaps a migration, perhaps... well, who knew? She'd talked, sometimes, about going back, when the time was right. When Ashé had modernised itself. (I wouldn't have said that criterion had been met, but she may have thought differently. Her own disagreement with the strictures of our birth society had been less fundamental, less visceral than my own. She had not made peace with Ashé, had left because of what she *thought*. I had left it because of what I *was*.)

There were forty-two thousand, two hundred and seventy-one names on the passenger manifest, another nine hundred listed as crew. Why did hers have to be among them?

The waltz winds to a close, and the dancers retreat into the shadows. From the corner of my vision, I note the figure shuffling its way closer to me, along the bench. I turn, but it is not the face I expect to see. Guilt has made way, for now, for the attentions of another.

'We need to talk,' says Grief.

The ship I currently control is an astonishing vessel, incredibly muscled, inordinately fast. And yet nowhere near fast enough. Space is immensely big, even the modest pockets of space which, candle-like, are lit by the flame of some small star, around which humans have chosen to congregate. At speeds unimaginable to all but the most recent of my ancestors, I crawl towards the place where my sister may or may not be.

This is not as it was supposed to be. I am not equipped, not prepared.

The things which, mere hours ago, made this a game – a sad game with dreadful undertones, but a game nonetheless – have evaporated, shadows melted away in the glare of an awful searchlight. There are things about the disaster – apparent disaster – with which I hadn't bothered to familiarise myself, because I didn't need to know.

I need to know.

I become obsessed with the few known facts of the *Bougainvillaea*'s disappearance.

The ship, a Borken III / Notocero Delta cryoberth passenger vessel leased to AdAstra Migrations, had been en route from the habitats of Tau Ceti to the terraform project of HIP 56948, an altspace transit of some three-plus weeks. But the transit had aborted, for no known reason. A bald mayday signal, yielding the vessel's ident and a minimal summary of its status – CAD drive inoperative, main transmitter destroyed, lifesystems still functional – had been received two weeks ago at Eps Eri, seventeen daycycles after the *Bougainvillaea*'s altspace departure from Tau Ceti. Multiple detections of the distress signal were reported: it was picked up first by a mining vessel journeying to the Jotunheim trojans, and subsequently by receivers on Ashé itself, at the Ashé-L5 observatory, and at the small interdiction garrison stationed at Utgard. The photonic signal was too weak and too transient to pinpoint directly, but precise timing of the signal's arrival at the various detection points yielded a location for the signal's origin which was, surprisingly, within the outer system of Eps Eri itself. The altspace transit time between Tau Ceti and Eps Eri was a matter of mere hours, which implied that the *Bougainvillaea* had lain fallow, undetected, stricken, within – at most – a light-hour of Ashé for sixteen whole daycycles before it had so briefly managed to announce itself.

And all subsequent attempts to make contact with, and to intercept, the *Bougainvillaea* had failed utterly. Ashé's space-rescue specialists knew where the ship was, or had been, mere hours before, but they could not find it.

The salvage teams, sniffing blood or at least opportunity, moved in. Alongside Ashé's own salvage crews, the more entrepreneurial and ruthless of Tau Ceti's wrecked-spacecraft specialists had gathered, alerted to the developing situation by the news carried on a scheduled commercial altspace flight between Eps Eri and Tau Ceti. It took several days longer before another ship brought the news to Sol, and to Borken Corporate's headquarters.

Lifesystems still functional. I would cling to the promise of this simple code, but for the terrible conundrum that is the coin's other side: if the 43000-odd passengers and crew of such a large passenger vessel are still alive, and somewhere within Ashé's local zone of influence, *where are they*?

Where, in particular, are Nasreen and her family?

three

'Oh, sure, Borken makes it happen. But this—she gestures with her arm, as though to encompass the foyer and corridor—'this is all Notocero. That's the magic of it.'

'But you must concede,' argues "Toyah", 'that you left a lot of people very disappointed. And not just me.'

'I didn't—'

She was never one to hear someone out – was always more convinced of the wisdom of her own thoughts than anything anyone else could come up with – and this "Toyah" has that aspect of the original well-and-truly captured. I am, despite myself, once again believing, as K@rine, still in character, continues. 'I don't mean in a physical sense, because longer-term that's not that important. And I don't even mean in an emotional sense. What I mean is, in a *moral* sense. You let people down, left right centre. You cut and ran, Char.'

'That supposed to be some kind of wordplay?'

'You never gave Ashé the chance.'

'I gave plenty—'

'Not post-changeover, you didn't. It was just "Look, new me, I'm leaving".'

'That's *so* un— dammit, Toy, you know full well the kind of shit I'd been going through. And might I point out—'

'You ever think,' asks "Toyah", 'about the opportunity you had to help change society?'

'*Chickenshit* change society! I couldn't even change *you*, Toy. What was it you said, that night I tried to talk to you?'

'If you expect me to recall the things I said a generation ago, Char, I... okay, curious, what was it I said?'

'You said I couldn't have made a worse mess if I—'

"Toyah" interjects again. 'I was angry. I mean, put yourself in my shoes.'

'Your shoes? *Your* shoes? My horn-headed god, how can you say that? If I'd just *once* had the sense that someone else was making the effort to try and see what I saw, what I felt... but you never did. You never did. None of you.'

'You never gave us the chance, Char. And I was angry, that night, I was furious, I felt betrayed... I mean, suddenly it turns out my boyfriend is now a g—'

'Like I tried to explain, I *had* to. I wasn't right, as things were. I *never felt right*. And you never bothered to notice.'

'You can hardly blame me for that.'

'Why the hell not? You're pretty free with the blame yourself. Always were.'

'Because, as it turns out, you cut and ran. You could've stood up for what you believed in.'

'And provide more martyr material? Gee, no thanks, Toyah.' I stroke my chin, as though searching out stubble, and suddenly I'm panicking about where this has brought me. I've had several lovers since Toyah, am faced here with a representation of her which doesn't capture the look, nor even the sound, yet still somehow convinces… and I'm surprised at my mental state, at the not-altogether-welcome degree of arousal that's unfurled itself, unbidden. She wouldn't approve; and I'm not sure I do either. 'Quit,' I say.

And simple as that, "Toyah" is gone, and it's just K@rine again. 'Was that… accurate?' it asks.

I'm not ready to reply straightaway.

It's a strange gig, this relationship between android and pilot. It arises from the need to communicate, across interplanetary distances, and not to be forever beholden to the slowness of photons. Transit time, each way, for radio communication between *Peregrinator*'s present position and the ships in the *Bougainvillaea* search zone is currently around ten minutes. The circumstances of my need to contact the dozen ships of the search effort are rather unusual, but the problem is by no means unique: humans haven't evolved to cope with regular multi-minute delays between each exchange in a conversation. Which is where proxies come in, to afford at least the simulacrum of spontaneous dialogue, unfettered by delay; but a transmitted proxy is only as good as its adherence to its human template. Related to which is the question of trust. K@rine's negative-space approach to "template personality research" is admittedly unorthodox, but over the months I've known it, I have come to appreciate that K@rine is very good at what it does.

The proxies we will need here will require meticulous construction, not least because I do not wish my current unease – this numbing, congealed feeling which rides my heart – to leak through into my alter egos. I spend a couple of hours discussing with K@rine the issues on which I place primary importance, I get it to run through a simulated transmission with me – and am faced with the curious, unsettling phenomenon of playing devil's advocate with *myself*, struggling to catch "myself" out in some reaction or other. At length I concede that K@rine's work on these proxies cannot be faulted. They are, in every necessary respect, very like me. They *are* me; but armour-plated, sure-footed. They feel no pain. I envy them.

I give permission for their transmission, wondering what fate will befall each one.

This still leaves the proxy which must be constructed for transmission to Wlodek. I have been putting this one off.

There are twenty-odd copies of the proxy, most near-identical, that have been disseminated. Some have gone to various local bureaucratic departments, which have not requested contact from me but which, from experience, I know will take official umbrage should I not provide them with details of *Peregrinator*'s mission. Then there are the dozen ships of the search effort: the Ashé mil vessels *Victory Through Prudence*, *Catechism*, *Parlous Heroics*, *Small But Mighty*, and *Last Refuge*; the local civilian DSSAR ships *Succour in Adversity*, *Unstinting Vigilance*, and *Fortitude*; the Tau-Ceti-system salvage vessels *Slithy Tove*, *Kokopelli*, and *Now Just Cut That Out*; and the Gliese-65-registered rockminer *Torosaurus*.

I don't expect more than a cursory response from the mil ships, towards whom the purpose of proxy transmission is more to ensure that they have sufficient data to recognise me as friend, or at least authorised neutral entity, rather than foe. It's on the outsystem salvage ships that I will most keenly press for acknowledgement. Flightsystem information is keenly sought by Borken's competitors in the fields of deep-space engineering and altflight, and could be sold off rather than passed on to the relevant authorities. Indeed, it's probable that the salvage scows themselves are here at the behest of one or other of Borken's rivals, with the salvage ships' Tau Ceti registry providing a convenient layer of disguise. It's likely their sponsors are based elsewhere: perhaps Kerguelen-Anodyne operating out of Proxima Centauri system, or Hyperion/Kratos/Zenit from Wolf 359, both of whom have been hungry to break into Borken's market as a shipbuilder. So the proxies transmitted to the salvage vessels have been programmed with an acute understanding – significantly greater, in truth, than my own – of the legal avenues available to Borken should their recipients feel disinclined to pass on to us our due, or worse, consort with our corporate enemies.

Such pressure might be sufficient to encourage the salvors' cooperation, or it might not. *Peregrinator*'s speedy passage towards the search zone is another component of the same message; and while our ship is not armed, it does have the look, and the motive power, of a military vessel.

What happens, if the salvage ships find something? Well, that depends…

… but I will not fall apart. For my part, for Nasreen's sake, I will not fall apart.

*

There is less time than I had anticipated, before I am hailed. Oddly, it is none of the search vessels. Even more oddly, it is not a proxied conversation, transmitted back for my benefit; it is live.

It is Wlodek.

It is Anders Wlodek, who should still be in Utgard's vicinity, at a distance of three hundred million kilometres plus change from *Peregrinator*'s current position, and getting further every second. Yet he has initiated a direct ship-to-ship transmission, which at his position implies a communication time delay of 40 minutes. I have just time to register the inconsistency of what is happening, before K@rine, without waiting for my signal, patches him through. Full visual.

I'm conscious of my dishevilled, *g*-force-harried appearance, at the same time as I take in Wlodek's chiselled nose, pinched mouth, rheumy eyes. A face on which anger is awkwardly held in check.

'This is the *Peregrinator*? Is this Mertz?' Wlodek's voice is higher-pitched than his face would suggest; brassy; stern. I wait a few seconds to see if there is more to his questioning – it's customary to adopt batch mode, over long transmission lag times – but there isn't.

'Mertz here,' I reply, sweat pricking my palms. I start mentally counting off from my response. *Peregrinator*, or K@rine, can give me information about his distance from us; but I need these details *now*. While giving away as little as possible myself. 'Wlodek – Anders – my apologies. *Peregrinator*'s emergence wasn't where we were expecting. I judged the projected rendevzous at Utgard would prove… inefficient, in light of reaching the search zone. I would be happy to—'

The tic – the facial twitch which Wlodek gives, betraying my words' arrival – occurs only fifteen seconds, by my reckoning, from the start of my utterance. Just two million kilometres, a cosmic stone's throw. *How is this possible?* 'This is not acceptable,' says Wlodek. 'The arrangement was to transfer in Ashé local space, and you have summarily— what do you mean, *rendezvous at Utgard?*'

'I was told Utgard,' I reply, testily. 'So I was expecting Utgard. I will have the ship send you the details.'

'Mertz. This is not acceptable,' Wlodek repeats, after another quarter-minute pause. His brow creases, his lips grow thin. 'Cease acceleration forthwith, and make ready for ship-to-ship docking. Once you kill your thrust, my singleship should be able to make interception with you in no more than one daycycle. You have umbilical?'

'Wlodek... Anders, I do not see what difference it makes, at this point, who is in command of *Peregrinator*. My priority is clearly to ensure that we – that is, *Peregrinator* – reach the search zone as rapidly as possible. Lives are at stake, many lives. A day's coasting is an unwarranted delay—'

'*Do not see what difference!*' He takes a couple of seconds, it seems, to moderate his voice, and continues more slowly, more controlled. 'I would advise you, Pilot Mertz, to heed your instructions. You are playing a dangerous game here. A very dangerous game. The instructions were clear, and I insist – it is not your concern to assess priority. I want the *Peregrinator*. I have command of the mission... and now you say *unwarranted?*' The aggression he places on this last word is frightening.

I do not have time for this. 'Wlodek. I suggest you return to Ashé. I will keep you informed of the mission's progress. But I have a job to do. Mertz out.'

I butt my fingertips against my upraised palm, and K@rine cuts the transmission. Wlodek's visage dissolves from the screen, leaving a ghostly, apoplectic afterimage when I close my eyes.

I pull a water bulb from the crash-couch's armside locker, take a couple of gulps. I note, belatedly, that my brow is slick with perspiration, and my hands are shaking. 'K@rine, how is this possible?' I ask. 'Wlodek, here, I mean? Surely he would not have altspaced between Utgard and Ashé, the cost would be ludicrous… and why did you open the transmission in the first place?'

'Charmain, I did not,' it replies. 'It would appear pilot Wlodek was using an override code to initiate the communication.' Its wooden face is as expressionless as ever, and yet somehow I think I see contrition in its posture.

'Then block it, in future. I don't want to have to speak to him unprepared. And – two million kay-emm, that's not even Ashé, with the distance we've put behind us. He mentioned a singleship. Do you have its position?'

'Pilot Wlodek's singleship is almost directly astern. It is, as you suggest, slightly more than two million kilometres in our wake. Do you require a precise location?'

'No, K@rine. I just need to know roughly where he is – and whether he can catch us.'

'Without knowing the exact specifications of his singleship, I cannot be sure.'

'The transmission handshaking didn't include an ident?'

'No.'

'That in itself is worrying.' I purse my lips. 'Can we get a visual? Find out what he's running?'

'I have already been making the attempt. He's still too far astern to get a view of sufficient quality through RF imaging, and the drive plasma has been interfering with the lidar measurements. Do you wish me to cut boost, Charmain? An hour should be sufficient to derive an accurate silhouette for pilot Wlodek's vessel.'

'No. Let's keep kicking it until we need to coast. But you should at least have his velocity and delta-vee, right?'

'Velocity is ninety-eight point five kilometres per second.'

'So he's falling behind.'

'True, for now. But his acceleration profile is harder than ours. As he suggests, he can overtake us within one daycycle should we cease acceleration. And at present trends, even if we maintain thrust, he could close within five daycycles.'

'Is that likely? In just a singleship?'

There's a flash of something like concern on K@rine's wooden face; or I may just be projecting. 'I cannot discount it, though I concede it would be... unusual. There is a suggestion of structural irregularity in the RF imaging's best-fit silhouette. It appears to be larger than expected for a standard singleship. One interpretation would be that the vessel has had auxiliary drive units added. And the tenor of pilot Wlodek's recent communication suggests a certain single-mindedness on the subject of—'

'OK, then let's run hotter,' I reply. '*Peregrinator* still has its mil engines, correct? We can double our delta-vee, easy.'

'That's correct, Charmain. But the *g*-forces—'

'We'll cope.'

'And once we exceed seven hundred kps, the dangers from dust impacts—'

'I'm not talking about taking us over the seven-hundred limit, K@rine, just getting us up to that velocity sooner. And braking more abruptly, if it comes to that. As long as it doesn't smear me in the process. Or get the Ashé mil contingent overexcited.'

'Pilot Wlodek might still be able to intercept—'

'He'd have to be bloody stubborn to persist that far. That's got to put us most of the distance to the search zone, right? Even if he has the capability to close by then. I think he'll call off, if he has any sense.' *And if he doesn't, by that point he'll have an audience.*

I have no idea what Wlodek is playing at; but it's not, I judge, concern for the *Bougainvillaea* that's pushing him on.

In any case, I'm in no mood for his games.

Two responses to my set of requests arrive within an hour of my transmissions, scarce delayed at all save for the photons' round-trip crawl across several AUs distance. The *Fortitude*'s comms & liaison officer, one Lise Scherfig, is a young and sparely-built woman – short hair, pale skin, dark eyes, loose-fitting black clothing. She copies to us the dialogue initiated by my proxy: it's a two-minute meeting, across a plain desk in a sparsely-furnished room, which quickly confirms the cooperation of her vessel and of its DSSAR sister ships, the *Unstinting Vigilance* and the *Succour in Adversity*.

The *Torosaurus*' operator, Hieronymous Creasey is short but broad, balding yet swarthy, his face dominated by overly bushy eyebrows that threaten to amalgamate above the bridge of his nose. He has replied with a rambling vid burst which is as much guided tour of his ship, for my proxy's benefit, as it is response to my request.

I smile to myself, pegging Creasey as one of those too-garrulous types not fully suited to the isolated existence of the lone spacer. In an outsystem accent, most probably Delta Pav, the *Torosaurus'* captain offers in-principle support but also reminds me that since the mining ship is not officially engaged in the search effort, he is not anticipating having anything to report to me.

Tracking through a surprisingly well-equipped galley, he offers a hope that my mission is successful; turning first into a corridor and then into a broad, blue-themed rec lounge, he says that he has been praying for the welfare of those aboard the *Bougainvillaea*. This last strikes me as an incongruity: I suspect Creasey is wearing religion as an affectation, a common and successful strategy among outsystem businesspeople and workers when dealing with Eps Eri. (In contrast, the *Fortitude*'s Scherfig – local, therefore much more likely to be a believer of some description – provides no hint of such in her clipped, almost blunt transmission.)

An hour drags past, and I grow fretful. It's late in my diurnal cycle. I allow that I might, possibly, be tired.

I sleep, fitful, wretched; our acceleration is too heavy, my limbs ache, and my mind is pulled in a dozen directions. My sister, helplessly adrift in the limitless void of space, sometimes suited, sometimes lacking even that protection. Wlodek, furious, in pursuit. A vessel reduced by some unfathomable tragedy to far-flung shrapnel, or intact but tomb-like. A find, reported, distorted, or concealed. A nightmare, a nest of possibilities, none of them good.

When what passes for rest has ceased, I rise, raw-eyed. K@rine informs me that there is no news of significance from the search region, and that Wlodek's singleship, though closing, is still four daycycles or more from catching us. Nothing from my nightmare, then, has materialised. So why do I feel that the stakes have been raised while I slept?

The cabin feels cold, my goosefleshed limbs heavy. But it's more than just the lethargy of the newly-awakened that is running through me right now. I worry at my ability to bring this through.

Deep-system passenger ships have a certain size and shape, dictated by the conflicting requirements of the CAD field actuators, of the need for acceleration across urspace, and of humanity's dependence on something which, if not gravity *per se*, at least feels like gravity. (The cryopassengers are oblivious to such concerns, of course, but the warm ones, who are invariably wealthy, are *fussy*.) Vessels are broad enough for a flavour of spin-grav that minimises the spoilerish effects of coriolis, but not so distended as to threaten the structure's integrity on the transitions between urspace and altspace. All of which, plus the obligatory running lights and beacons, should mean that a ship such as the *Bougainvillaea* is sufficiently bulky for detection at a distance of only one AU, let alone the much smaller distances dictated by a well-resourced search-and-discover mission within a reasonably narrowly-defined target area. That such detection had not, in several days, occurred indicated that what had befallen the *Bougainvillaea* was... unusual. No ship. No wreckage. No hint, no signal, no beacon beyond that frustratingly brief squawk detected by the *Torosaurus* and the various ground stations, too many days ago.

The most benign explanation, severely problematic in itself (especially since the vessel's last status signal indicated insufficient materials for such an occurrence) is that the *Bougainvillaea* had somehow re-entered altspace and had subsequently reemerged into urspace, more than two weeks late, at her intended destination of HIP 56948. This possibility cannot be ruled out for the next few daycycles, until the projected arrival of the Tau-Ceti-bound freight vessel *Cumulus* brings the latest news from the terraform project. Perhaps the *Bougainvillaea* had even emerged somewhere else. But the problem with all these hypotheses was that no trace of CAD residue had been reported from the search region. The least benign explanation… could be very dark indeed.

The salvage crews, I suspect, have been hoping for dark, but not *too* dark.

(I'm not even daring to hope, not really. Not for my sister, her son, and her partner. There's too much hurt, and too much distance.)

While spin-grav tilts for "large", pursuit throws another variable into the equation. Acceleration – and, more generally, manoeuvrability – requires mass minimisation and robustness combined, which means that an ex-mil vessel such as *Peregrinator* has much more the needle-like profile of what was thought, by the primitives, to typify a spacecraft. It has its advantages: there aren't too many other altspace-capable vessels out there which can push 9 g when they need to. But when it's not under boost, the spin-grav is tawdry, and clunky with coriolis.

I'm tempted to run the craft under boost for still longer: but there is no sound navigational rationale for such a course, and plenty of good reasons to give the overheating linacs a rest. So, while *Peregrinator* reconfigures its cramped living-spaces for spin-grav, and while K@rine takes point duty at the controls of the collision-aversion station, I retire to my couch to fend off, for as long as possible, the coriolis headache which I know to be lying in wait.

Rest, perhaps; no sleep. The *Bougainvillaea* is a looming absence, a small and mysterious void within the immensity of Ashé's modest pocket of the Galaxy's vastness. The distance we traverse is a pittance, something which our photons could scale in less time than it took me to convince that imbecile Demetriodes of our *bona fides*, and yet it will still take us more than a week to reach the search region. Such delays are, of course, mere part-and-parcel: too small to justify the severe and haphazard expense of an alt-hop, too short for cryo, too long to meaningfully invest in preparation, or maintenance, or any of the other tasks which the ship's machines are, in any event, best equipped to tackle amongst themselves. And so I rest. And sim, and exercise, and... sim.

Time passes. What waits for us?

Another set of responses has come through. I feed the residue of my meal – protein strips, extruded vegetables, unconvincing noodles – into the san-chute, and move across to the message board. In short order, the meetings of my proxies with officials from the *Parlous Heroics*; the *Catechism*; the *Small But Mighty*; the *Last Refuge* and the *Victory Through Prudence* are received, promising cooperation and a free exchange of all pertinent information. The affirmation is close to meaningless – the Ashéan mil vessels will provide copies of the flight data, ultimately, as they are required by law to do; but I fully expect that should the *Bougainvillaea*'s wreckage come to light through their efforts, there will be a degree of stonewalling while the intel is sifted for any scraps of strategic military or technical advantage. (The same may also be true of the DSSAR ships whose despatches I received earlier, of course.) Nonetheless, it's a reassurance, and as much as I could have expected.

Having reviewed the mil ships' terse, templated replies – I smell a committee – I'm left wondering how long it will be before I hear back from the salvage vessels themselves.

There are none of the taupes and greys, the severe lighting, the utilitarian edges and planes that dominate the workaday spacecraft with which I normally associate. The foyer proclaims that this is a passenger vessel, appointed in moody and I suspect fashionable colours, fitted out with an eye to comfort, aspiring to suggest a restrained opulence. The corridor lighting is diffuse, as though I walk through a softly glowing nimbus; the ballroom chandeliers proud in their ability to catch the eye. It is a vast ship, mesmerising, overwhelming... deserted.

Though I pace down corridor after curved corridor, there is no sign of life, nothing but the thrum and sigh of the ship's omnipresent automated lifesystems to punctuate the stillness, the silence. I keep longing to catch sight, around some corner, up another spiralling rampway, across some arena or thoroughfare, of Nasreen, or of her son Ahmed, or of Jian, the brother-in-law I have never yet seen (and likely now never will), but this simulation is unpopulated. And even thus – knowing that I am engaged in mere virtual exploration – the experience feels confronting, as though I am scaling the ribcage of some vast phantom. This ship has limits, hard, immutable, an encasement from the surrounding vacuum, and yet it feels as though it extends without definition, as though I could find myself trapped here, wandering endlessly, and never find an escape.

And nobody is here.

Nasreen is not here. I tell myself she never was. Yet the passenger manifest proclaims otherwise.

I should be with her. Fumbling, I pull off the mask, blink in the disappointing glare of *Peregrinator*'s rec module, and resolve not to put myself through this again. I sit up, slouch forward, rest my face in the palms of my cupped hands, allow my grief an outlet.

Some minutes later, I wipe my eyes, breathe deep. It has not helped, the sim. It has not explained anything, it has not provided any new tangible connection with Nasreen. And it beggars belief, now I have experienced the scale of the ship for myself, that the search teams have not reported the minutest physical trace of the vanished *Bougainvillaea*.

'*They're dead; they're all dead.*' Unbidden. I've heard those words before, but where?

four

'It's the geometry. Solve the geometry, and you'll find your sister.'

I have no idea who the voice belongs to: K@rine, some ghost from my past, or perhaps Nasreen herself. The dream is over before I can discern this detail. It leaves me sweating, my heart hammering, for no identifiable reason. I wait out the dark until the terror passes.

The *Now Just Cut That Out* has issued a reply to our request for cooperation. It is a mere five-word snippet: 'We will, of course, comply.'

Offhand; and a touch ambiguous. And slow. It's taken just over a daycycle to get this response. Unlikely to be attributable to concern over getting the wording just-so; instead, the timing is remarkably suggestive of an altspace signal transmission, at 3.39 parsecs per daycycle, there-and-back to Tau Ceti. Which means: they're probably not a rival, as such. Tau Ceti hosts plenty of local manufacturing, but bulk-scale shipbuilding isn't one of their industries. If the time delay is an indication that Tau Ceti is pulling the *Now*'s strings, then the most likely employer is AdAstra itself, the *Bougainvillaea*'s owner and operator. (In which case, why so curt, why so slow in responding to the shipbuilder? Does AdAstra know something, or suspect something, about the *Bougainvillaea*'s disappearance that isn't common knowledge among the search parties?)

From their terseness, I doubt that they'd welcome further query. We shall see.

'Shave me,' I bid K@rine.

'How short?' it asks on arrival in my quarters. It holds an old-fashioned nanoblade trimmer in slim mahogany fingers.

'Eight mil,' I respond, looking at where K@rine's eyes would be.

'Is this chair sufficiently comfortable?'

'It'll pass.'

The shave is a process which could be completed in one minute, and there is no good reason for it to be more protracted. But K@rine takes almost half an hour; and, knowing K@rine and its idiosyncracies, its conceits, I do not press the matter. The touch of wooden fingers against my scalp – the precise, carefully tempered touch – is hypnotic, a little soporific, the throaty buzz of the trimmer almost illicit. If it is not, in truth, what I need right now, it is as fair a facsimile as I can reasonably expect.

I have long had cause to doubt K@rine's protestations of ignorance in the field of human interaction, and this trimming session provides yet more evidence.

But the memory of touch ebbs, is gone; and time remains.

Do I understand CAD drive theory? No, of course not. Have I been exposed to it? Naturally. I'd put it in the exact same bin in which I place astrology, alchemy, spiritualism… except, CAD *works*. That's enough for me.

It would not be enough for everybody. There are, I know, the grow-your-own-meat types, the ones who say you shouldn't use any tech you can't follow from first principles: I'm not of that number. Which is not saying I haven't tried to understand it, and I've seen enough exploded diagrams of CAD actuators, enough equation-infested explanations of the precise geometry required for the actuator's indium-113 payload, enough handwavy explanations of where the indium *goes* when the surrounding ship steps back out of altspace… if it was going to take hold in me, to make any coherent sense with its talk of alt-spatial-hypergeometric-affinity, pseudoquantised-excitation-of-bulk-matter, indefinitely-prolonged-resonance and all the rest, then by now it would have done so. And it hasn't. I can live with that. I don't need to *know* whence the three point three nine parsecs per day speed limit arises, it's just useful to know that it operates. But it does make the *Bougainvillaea*'s disappearance the more mysterious.

Where is the *Bougainvillaea* now?

It's the central question, the obvious dilemma. Dead in the water – fundamentally intact, but radio-quiet? Unlikely: the search teams would have found it by now. Kicked somehow into a high-velocity hyperbolic trajectory, so that by the time it was sought, it had already escaped the search cordon? Implausible: while the fringes of CAD theory involve some vaguely weird physics, it isn't thought possible to violate the principle of urspace conservation-of-momentum, which would dictate she'd be moving slow unless she'd been deliberately placed under high boost for an extended period. Smashed to flinders in some collision with one of Eps Eri's comparatively plentiful orbiting rockpiles?

Superficially feasible: but a collision so large, so violent, would have been detected by numerous observatories distributed throughout the system, and even an implausibly energetic explosion would have strewn some easily detectable IR-bright fragments, if nothing else. So far as I know, there have been no indications of any such fragments, no material traces whatsoever. (Of course, it is possible that one of the salvage scows may have chanced on something, but I am confident that Ashé's mil fleet will be keeping at least one predatory eye on each of the salvage ships, alert to the possibility of unauthorised action...)

Which leaves the other hunches, the more creepy notions that *Bougainvillaea* was here, but now is gone... somewhere unknowable. If she'd slipped back into altspace, and perhaps hasn't yet re-emerged (*might never re-emerge*, is the thought I strive to keep from bubbling up to the surface), then we will probably never find her. It's not automatically a hopeless thought: even if its altspace transit takes the *Bougainvillaea* beyond the ken of human urspace, it may eventually emerge in some system which the inhabitants can colonise. Starships are designed to be closed systems, after all, and to recycle their resources efficiently... but a passenger liner does not carry all the apparatus of a proper colony ship, could not succeed on its own in transplanting twenty-sixth-century human civilisation in a completely new system. Such hope might, thus, be false, merely a slow death. And it's doubtful whether *Bougainvillaea* would have been capable, after signalling at Eps Eri, of transitioning again to altspace. The timing of its arrival at Eps Eri was already problematic, and best explained by a flight path which had already brought it, doglegged to an extreme, from Tau Ceti in two hops. Liners typically carried a spare aliquot of In-113; they didn't generally carry *two* spare allotments.

Which implied that the *Bougainvillaea* had already made its two jumps by the time she arrived here.

She should still be here.

She isn't here, or is concealed excessively well.

I will never see her again.

What am I to make of Occam's razor, when none of the blades will fit?

'I'm curious,' says "Dafydd". 'What did it feel like, when you had it done?'

This is in keeping: amongst my circle, Dafydd was always the prurient one, the sleaze, the player-with-innuendo. If any of them were to make so bold as to ask me that question, it would be him. And again, K@rine, with neither his height nor his bulk to work with, captures some nuance of him with eerie fidelity.

'What did it feel like?' I retort. 'Try for yourself, see what you think.' I'm playing for time. Wondering what K@rine's angle is this time. Wondering if it *has* an angle.

'Don't be like that,' "Dafydd" replies. 'It's just… you did this, and you never bothered to explain to any of us. Fair enough, in one sense, but you could've given us the chance.'

'Daf, I'm tired,' I say. Which is true enough. The waiting, the tension… it's draining. K@rine's role-plays pass the time, well enough, but they also seem designed to provoke, to unsettle at a time when I would have thought I could do without any provocation beyond the immediacy of the *Bougainvillaea*'s unfolding and mysterious disaster.

'But, alright, if you must: Weird. Right. Sore. Scary. And I could've done with some fucking *support*.'

'You shunned it. Never sought it. Couldn't see it when it was offered.'

'That's *not true*!' I reply, voice ramped up too much. Shaking, hands clenched. Questioning, even while I make the assertion.

'Isn't it? You were always about being the odd one out, being so fucking different, never bothered to see what me, Mig, Toy, the rest of us all saw in you. Fine, this was something you needed to do, I *get* that. Pretty sure we all did. But you didn't have to just cut us off the way you did.'

'Daf, I didn't *cut you off*. I *left Ashé*, because that was what needed to happen. You know what the prevailing attitudes were to – to people like me.'

'Prevailing?' asks "Dafydd". 'Yeah, but even then, things were chan—'

'Oh, *birdcrap* they were changing. I left because I had no desire to be turned into some kind of poster child for gender deviance, and if you can't fathom that, you've got a worse case of selective memory than I thought.'

'Carlos – Charmain – we were your *friends*. *I* was your friend. And maybe more than that, if you'd allowed it.'

'What the hell do you mean by "maybe more than that"?' I ask.

'I would've had you like that,' says "Dafydd". 'If you'd been interested.'

I exhale slowly, pause. 'That was... uh, never on the cards. I mean, you know you're not my type. Besides, I hardly even saw you post-op, before I left.'

'I *wasn't talking* about post-op.'

I open my mouth; nothing emerges. I realise, after several seconds, that I'm simply staring at the woodgrained face of a machine. I make a grimace of the gesture of closing my mouth, not knowing what to say. Because what K@rine has intimated about Dafydd is true; correct; I can taste the validity behind it, on my memories. His way of thinking, all the time I'd known him, had been every bit as forbidden as my own. And I'm stunned at the realisation that *I must have known, myself,* on some level, but had kept it submerged all this time. Even from myself.

'Quit?' K@rine asks, eventually.

It's four days since I cast my flock of proxies to the heavens, and replies have now come in from all the vessels save the third salvage ship, the *Slithy Tove*. Most recent to answer has been the *Kokopelli*, from which I've received a straightforward avowal of cooperation. The ninety-odd-hour delay in this response could mean anything, and I'm not tempted to read any particular message into the timing: if the *Kokopelli* has out-system backers (and it's a strong bet that they do), at least they appear unwilling to make things awkward for Borken. (Although an assurance given does not guarantee a commitment delivered…)

It hurts more than I would have expected.

A simple public-access-data search reveals that Dafydd, two months my junior, died five years ago. A low-altitude vehicle accident: failure of the collision avoidance system, mountainous terrain, heavy fog. There is no reason anyone would have thought to inform me, even if they had known how to contact me; but Eps Eri has just grown that bit colder.

I do not rise from my seat for many minutes.

Later, K@rine informs me that Wlodek, whose ship is now steadily gaining on us (at a velocity that I would consider reckless in such a dusty environment, in a vessel presumably lacking mil armour), is again seeking to make contact with me.

I decline. I do not wish to speak to that man. But it is to no avail; for he once again has found a path through our comms' defences.

'Mertz?'

'Anders,' I reply. 'Former pilot Wlodek. I believe that I had indicated my reasons for not attempting rendezvous with you. My mission has always been—'

He interrupts; the lightspeed delay is under ten seconds. 'You are making a mistake bigger than you realise, Pilot Mertz. You will be *finished* with Borken before this is done.'

'Is that a threat, former pilot Wlodek? Because I've got a ship to find, and you're just *getting in my way*.'

'Mertz. I demand that you cooperate. As the senior Borken representative in this region, I—'

I tune out his rant, compose my reply. 'I repeat, I've given you my reasons. *Peregrinator*'s mission is to use every means necessary to help locate the *Bougainvillaea*. I don't see what possible justification there could be for insisting on a personnel transfer which seems only guaranteed to impede our progress to the search region.'

He has paused in his tirade before I complete my response. I wait. Ten seconds.

'It is *not up to what you see*, Mertz. I am the senior Borken representative in this system. I will see you *finished*. I *demand*, I command that you—' There is spittle starting to collect at the corners of his mouth.

'I've heard enough. K@rine, kill the connect, please.' And I get up from my chair, leave the command station without checking whether K@rine has succeeded in disconnecting Wlodek's transmission.

I should worry about what Wlodek intends; because at current relative velocities, and considering the decel profile we will need to adopt as we approach the search windows, Wlodek will catch us. But I cannot, for the moment, take his threats seriously.

Besides, I have a plan. Or so I tell myself.

five

'They're leaving. Just like you did. Cutting and running.'

This voice, at least, I know: it's Toyah. And when I waken, it means something, but not straightaway.

Late on the fourth daycycle, among the base-level info-releases, there is a rumour. Observers believe Notocero to be making overtures for industrial collaboration with H/K/Z, the Wolf 359 deep-space heavy engineering and freight transport concern. It is, as speculation goes, not of particular note, although I can't help but be intrigued despite my longstanding indifference to the vagaries of intersystem finance and of industrial posturing.

A repositioning of this kind would be a major blow to Borken, which has built its reputation in large part on the hand-in-glove fit between its own impeccable propulsion systems and hi-vac heavy engineering, and Notocero's state-of-the-art lifesystems and resource recycling architecture. There is just enough play to the story, released across Ashé's public information system, to suggest the rumour may have some basis. In which case, the timing – during the most intense and sustained search ever for a missing or stricken Borken-Notocero passenger craft – is provocative, to say the least.

It's impossible to believe that the story's emergence, *now*, is mere coincidence.

Why would Notocero consider such an action? Do they know something Borken doesn't wish to be made public?

Secrets. There seem to be quite a few about.

I have some, too, of course. Even from K@rine.

I was, I think, twelve. Lying in my bed, in the customary cool of my family's forty-metres-depth dwelling, in one corner of the converted mine complex that was Medina, a cooberpedy excavated from a rocky promontory just south of the equator on Penitence's eastern shore. It was a winter's evening, the glow from our home's periscoped, brachiated skylight just starting to dim sufficiently to require artificial augmentation, though I was putting off issuing the command that would activate the glow-patches on my bedroom's ceramicised walls.

My hand was under my nightshirt, playing explorer.

It wasn't really a sexual thing, not consciously: I was still short, child-hipped, my voice unbroken. But I found it intriguing, this... trick. What I'd just discovered was that, by pressing down on the tip of my penis, at just the right angle, I could induce it to part-slide, part-fold back into my body, and could then hold it confined within the surrounding skin, the latter pulled across from left and right, squeezed up to form an ersatz vagina. (It would have been a rediscovery on my part, I think; I have a vague and unreliable recollection of similar manipulations, back from when I was four or five.) Now, when with my other hand I lifted up the bedsheet and the collar of my nightshirt and gazed down, I noticed – registered – that my groin looked like a girl's, pretty much. It felt... odd. And not completely comfortable.

But it made me smile.

Years later, sixteen, still at school. (Still at this stage Carlos, because of course as yet I lacked the autonomy, the wherewithal, and yes I suppose the guts, to become Charmain.) I was with a girl, Imogen: such things were expected of us, even though they were also frowned upon. (At sixteen, I had learned that life was to be a difficult and ill-defined balancing act. I don't think I've ever had reason, yet, to unlearn that.)

I can't remember if it was my room or hers. We were naked, but we weren't planning to go all the way because neither of us wished to jeopardise our immortal souls. And I showed her the penis-trick, more difficult to sustain now because I was older. I did it as a joke, thinking she'd see the funny side. She didn't.

The next week Antal, and later Gustav and Mohamed, started to call me "girl". I was stung by Imogen's betrayal, and by the fact that the boys regarded the label as an insult. And I tried to argue the point with them, which was, on reflection, unwise.

The last year of school was pretty rough.

Wlodek continues to gain, although he has at last commenced deceleration. His proximity, and the change in his vessel's attitude for braking, has allowed K@rine to obtain reliable imagery of the singleship, through a two-colour lidar scan.

"An old pilot is a cautious pilot": that should hold true across the dusty surrounds of Eps Eri, even more than elsewhere. And yet Wlodek, who must be at least fifteen years my senior, is not displaying anything approximating caution. His singleship lacks apparent ablative shielding, except for an ineffectual token sheath of nosecone; the six – six! – H/K/Z heavy-thrust plasma nacelles which ring the ship's central cylindrical lifechamber are pylon-mounted, rather than flared into the fuselage, presumably to permit them to run hotter without overswamping the layer of blindingly-bright refrigeration lasers that are clustered close against the vessel's main cylinder. The lifechamber has an axial length is almost fifteen metres, but is less than two metres in diameter: I doubt that Wlodek has room, inside, to even turn around, and the configuration does not lend itself to spin-grav. The docking collar is an awkward interruption in the layer of refrig lasers, and is visibly warmer (in false-colour IR) than the rest of the skin amidships. Overall, it's a vessel built for speed, not manoeuvrability. I could sum up its current deployment in two words: "death trap". If Wlodek is not completely insane, he is at least desperate.

There's another sense to the desperation, beyond the craft's reckless velocity. K@rine has calculated, from the vessel's dimensions, assumed laden mass, and the known characteristics of the H / K / Z heavies, that Wlodek must have expended at least forty-five percent of his total propellant in accelerating to his peak velocity, and will require almost as much again for complete deceleration. If he does not succeed in catching us, and against the odds does not succumb to the very real dangers of dust-grain impact (either to the lifechamber itself, or to one of the AM isolation pods), he is placing himself in very real risk of stranding, in a ship which likely only has rudimentary life-support capabilities.

I have no intention of allowing Wlodek to catch *Peregrinator*; nor can I fathom what may lie at the base of his haste.

In the wider context of the *Bougainvillaea*'s disappearance, also, something's not right.

I've known that from the outset. But the *what* of it... I spend fruitless hours interrogating *Peregrinator*'s mind, which contains the sum of public human knowledge and a good deal that is private. There's much on Borken, on CAD drive tech, on the forlorn history of previous altspace disasters and their urspace aftermaths, and on a dozen other possibly relevant topics. Interactions between Eps Eri, Tau Ceti, Sol ... There are *hundreds* of possible directions I could choose to explore. I could all too easily drown in a sea of data, without ever having espied a single useful clue.

If something's awry, then someone must have knowledge. So I trawl connections: Borken subsidiaries, associates, directors. Notocero's relationships with other concerns. I find puffery: "*The Borken III / Notocero Gamma is a design classic, a versatile, almost infinitely reconfigurable framework, a perfect symbiosis. Over seventy percent of migration events for the past three decades have utilised the B3Nγ's enviably reliable transport platform...*" Words that could be lifted from Borken's own promotional literature, regurgitated as unbiased journalistic opinion. Table after table of dry financial data, opaque in its professed objectivity, as good as meaningless to me. I find a typically tangled network of industrial collaborations, a smattering of lawsuits, a couple of class actions, official investigations, an unexplained delay in the release of the latest financial records, hints of inappropriate collusions, duopolistic high-handedness. None of it out of character for an aggressive, pseudo-imperialistic business organisation, none of it particularly surprising. None of it new.

None of it new. Well, there wouldn't be. Not over the past fortnight, at least. 'K@rine? What's the current local protocol for accessing mind-pool updates, beyond base-level?'

'There isn't one,' it replies. 'At least, not within trans-Ashéan space.'

'In this day and age? You're kidding me.'

'Regrettably, no. If we were on Ashé itself, as intersystem visitors, it would be a matter of making application to the Bur—'

'The Bureau of Information,' I say. 'Yes, I know *that*. But...'

'I gather that there are political factors which make the withholding of real-time mind-pool updates a matter of expedience, at this point. There is speculation that the local filtering of sensitive commercial or political information might be insufficiently reliable for free access. It's a circumstance that pre-dates the *Bougain*— the current situation by some months, and though it represents an escalation of prevailing Ashéan societal—'

In which case I'm mildly surprised that the Notocero collaboration rumour made the cut. 'Yes, alright,' I interrupt, testily. 'We're a society of backward-glancing suspicious bigots, I get the inference. I just... uh.'

'Apologies, Charmain. I did not anticipate you would take the observation personally.'

It caught me a little unawares myself. 'Shit.'

'Charmain?'

'I was really hoping I was going to be able to avoid this.'

'Charmain?'

'Who in the Bureau of Information would I need to approach, as an Ashéan citizen by birthright, seeking higher-level remote access privileges to the local public mind-pool?'

K@rine tells me.

'You are kidding me, right?'

She – it – is not kidding me. I need to think this through.

This is going to be painful. And not helped by the eighteen-minute transmission delay. But a proxy will not help me here.

I get the visual. He looks older than in my mind's eye – heavier at the jowls, wrinkles taking hold at the corners of his eyes. No grey yet. What I am seeing is merely a still image while he awaits my reply – there is no way he would stare into the viewer for eighteen unresponsive minutes. I have, nonetheless, instructed K@rine to send out my own image realtime, as an indication that, while he has other duties to which he must attend, this for me is the only game in play.

'Miguel,' I say, and despite myself, feel compelled to pause for his response. But to pause now would serve no purpose. The only way to do this, to conduct a meaningful conversation across a thousand-second round-trip time delay, is by conveying as much as possible in as few transmissions as can be exchanged. 'Miguel. I do not know if you remember me. But I remember you. I am presenting myself to you as Investigator Charmain Mertz, for that is who I am. But it is not who I was. When you knew me, a couple of decades ago now, you would have known me as Carlos Miyaki. And back then, I believe, you considered me to be a friend. I... feel that I betrayed that friendship, not by departing Ashé, because I stand by my reasons for doing that, but for leaving without informing you. I can well understand that this, for you, constituted a betrayal, and I am sorry for that. I am sorry. I cannot say that enough. I cannot expect you to accept that. But I must ask something of you, and I ask it as someone who grew up here, with all that that entails. Miguel, I need your help.'

I go on to describe my concerns about the *Bougainvillaea*'s fate, my feelings of powerlessness in the wake of Nasreen's disappearance, my suspicion that I might be missing important information – information within the public domain, or near enough, but which has not been included in the base-level data feed, nor in the specific operational updates that I have been receiving on salvage-team and search-vessel movements and the like. I finish up, rub my eyes. I am feeling as utterly drained as though I have been withstanding a 6 *g* acceleration slog, but it has taken me only five minutes to pour out my heart, to place my head on the block. I have wanted, but do not know how, to say something of Dafydd, to whom Miguel had been closer than I. But anything I might say on this would be inadequate – too late, irrelevant, too likely hurtful. I'll leave the wound unopened. On this occasion, at least.

And my opening words have not even *reached* Miguel yet.

I stare at the screen. His unchanging visage stares back. A dozen or more minutes later, and his face jumps, takes on a twitch of animation. Miguel blinks, he frowns, he breathes in. A scene of conflict plays out upon his face, to which my own responds in dumb mammalian instinct – as though there is any way my responses can, from his frame of reference, be seen to synchronise with his expression. He hears me out, and then he makes his reply. It is a lengthy reply, and not easy to listen to. Before the end of his second sentence, he is crying.

Before he finishes, and despite my best efforts, so am I.

I obtain the mind-pool access I am seeking. And, perhaps two decades late, I learn something of Miguel, and of friendship.

Five daycycles into the arc, and minutes after the fourth minor course correction in rapid succession – these tics and swerves will become more frequent as we near the inner belt – K@rine alerts me to a development in the search zone, still a half AU or more ahead of us. The *Slithy Tove* is powering up.

The activation of the *Slithy*'s attitude rockets is a commonplace enough occurrence. Within the comparatively crowded region of the search zone – a dozen ships, several significantly-sized asteroids, myriad smaller rocks, one unanswered question – ship movements are frequent, and necessary. The small gusts of directed plasma might indicate a change in cruise heading, a change in vessel orientation, a rejigging of spin-grav, a lazy-pilot method for infalling rock deflection. But this time, the reorientation is succeeded by a flaring of the *Slithy*'s main propulsion units, with every indication of a significant and protracted burn. This is no modest repositioning of a search asset. Someone is in a hurry.

What have they found?

The lack of chatter, the absence of any ship-to-ship context for the salvage vessel's movements, is maddening. I wait for anxious minutes, aware that the slow march of photons ensures that anything I learn of the *Slithy*'s motives, of its implications for the *Bougainvillaea*'s fate, will be several minutes stale for those in the search region. But this is, in some sense, a false concern. The burn proceeds; the *Slithy Tove* continues to accelerate. Soon enough, it becomes clear that she is leaving the search area behind. And not too many minutes later, there is the actinic burst characteristic of the salvage ship's awkward transition to urspace.

The *Slithy Tove* has packed up and gone home, with not a word of explanation.

There's a sum to all this, though I have no idea of the total, and perhaps no-one does. But: the *Bougainvillaea*'s continued absence, the *Slithy Tove*'s unexplained departure, the games which the Ashé media are playing, Wlodek's insistence on being in on the hunt, and now the industrial intrigue surrounding Notocero and H/K/Z. I'm not good with puzzles. But someone knows something which is being concealed from me.

Notocero has storefronts, factories, and research laboratories on Ashé, while Borken has only a slender commercial presence – scarcely more than Wlodek himself – at Eps Eri. Having so clearly wrong-footed Anders Wlodek, I cannot find the appetite to press him for information; nor do I consider it likely that he would give me any. Nor would I trust him.

Any other time, I'd regard the local Notocero presence as the natural conduit for details concerning the twinned corporations. But here, now… it's possible that Wlodek has already soured them against me, and even if not, I suspect Notocero would treat any query, from an acknowledged Borken representative, with the utmost suspicion. If I'm seeking information, background, to whatever has happened here, I'm unlikely to get help from them. And there's no meaningful way (short of re-entering altspace, which would mean abandoning the mission altogether) of contacting Borken's higher-ups.

I do not really know why, but I am on my own.

*

Sleep, yet again, is fitful, and scarce worth the effort. I wake with the taste of something rancid in my mouth – the edge of some misremembered dream, perhaps, or a glitch in *Peregrinator's* environmental systems. (It wouldn't be the first time.) K@rine is standing over me, shaking me awake.

'Status?' I ask.

'You asked to be alerted... News has come through from Tau Ceti, via the *Hellebore*. The *Cumulus*, in turn, has reported that the revised arrival window for the *Bougainvillaea*, at HIP 56948, has lapsed without any signal or sighting of the vessel.'

It's the news I'd been expecting. There wasn't realistically any hope that the *Bougainvillaea* could have made three alt-space hops, when she carried only sufficient In-113 for two. And yet it hits me like a bow-shock. I cannot find the impetus to rise from the cot.

Nasreen. Ahmed. Jian.

I'm given no time to absorb the news, because the comms signal is sounding. I make my way, still sleep-stumbling, to the command station, hoping that it is something important, something useful, something *good*.

It is not. It is Wlodek, who has once again managed to breach *Peregrinator's* communication filters. (*How many backdoors does this spacecraft's comms system have?*)

'Pilot Mertz! You must relent from this mutinous action! Kindly comply with my repeated instruction, with the direct orders given to you. You are to permit me to take command of the *Peregrinator*! Forthwith!'

'Mutinous, former pilot Wlodek? How so?'

I count off the seconds in my head: he grimaces at five, when my question reaches him. 'I am the rightful and recognised commander of this mission! Yet you continue to unlawfully withhold my vessel from me, while you spend your time in self-serving psychodramas with your android—'

I stop listening. His words have turned to ice in my ears. *How does he know about my sessions with K@rine?* 'Kill,' I say to K@rine, my voice trembling. Wlodek is cut off mid-diatribe.

'K@rine?' I ask. 'How does he know? And how has he been continuing to establish contact, against my instructions?'

'I… do not know, Charmain. Most likely there is an override in the comms system, of which I am not aware. There are checks I can run—'

'Do it. And reconnect him.'

'Reconnect?'

'I want to finish with the bastard.'

I am not even sure that Wlodek has noticed the disconnect, which in itself says something. 'This is beyond transgression! This is conduct inexcusable from a Borken employee! I demand that you decelerate the *Peregrinator* and permit me to take charge of the vessel! This is a *direct order*. Comply, Mertz, or I will break you. You should be in no doubt that—'

There is some aspect to the purity of his aggression, the clarity of his diction, which confirms a new suspicion. I tune out his rant. 'Tell me, former pilot Wlodek, do you like horses?'

At five he falls silent. Six. Seven. Eight. Nine, ten, eleven, twelve. At fifteen he replies: 'I do not understand the purpose of your question.'

'When did you last move your bowels? Do you consider that children these days show enough respect to their parents? Are you wearing grey undergarments, or white? Or, perhaps, none?'

These are not the responses from me he was expecting. Not the responses he was designed for. And he *cannot answer them*.

I turn my head. 'K@rine, please find a way to block this proxy's subsequent attempts to contact us. Even if it means taking the comms offline altogether. And disable whatever damned override this... *thing* has been using.' I get up: "Wlodek" is speaking again, as the screen dies.

So. We are being pursued by a singleship, piloted not by a human but by a proxy.

Which makes it, I suppose, nothing other than a missile...

six

'I don't see why you're complaining. You've taken plenty of pot shots at us, *over the years.'*

A recent bump in the price of In-113, suggesting an unusual purchasing pattern. A delay in the reporting of profits for Borken's Eps Eri subsidiary. Wlodek – who, to a large extent, *is* Borken at Eps Eri – not where he claims to be, and desperate to gain control of an altspace-capable vessel…

Why do I get the feeling these things are connected?

It's Daycycle Eight. I'm infusing the latest mind-pool updates. With the news from the *Cumulus*, that the *Bougainvillaea* has categorically not reached HIP 56948, there's been a spike in media speculation on the missing ship. And something jars. Such a bland detail that at first I don't notice… but it's there.

'It's unthinkable,' runs the quote from a local pundit, 'that a bee-three-enn-gamma intersystem passenger carrier would just… I mean, the idea that it's somehow made some kind of accidental and unforeseen retransition into alt-space, it goes against everything we know about the physics of the process, the failsafes that are engineered in. I mean, the layers of safeguard which would need to be circumvented, it's completely... I really cannot countenance that as an explanation. As to where the *Bougainvillaea* is now, I've no idea. But I can tell you where it's *not*, and that's altspace.'

Then, from my crash-couch berth, I query *Peregrinator*'s archive, and the doubt hits.

We are now a mere half a light-minute – ten million kilometres or so – from the edge of the increasingly ill-defined search zone, and continuing to pile on the *g* forces in deceleration. The Wlodek singleship is still – amazingly – in pursuit, and managing to match our deceleration profile for a rendezvous within the next half a daycycle. And while the singleship's trajectory yet remains potentially ballistic, there are other obvious concerns as it approaches. A plasma drive plume can inflict a lot of damage on a vessel, from a considerable distance.

There has been no further contact from "Wlodek". Which, hopefully, means that the override has been disabled. But I still have a threat to neutralise.

It must be closer to thirty years than twenty, since I last saw Xan.

'If there was anyone I did it for,' I say, 'other than of course for myself, that person would be you.'

"Xan" doesn't respond initially, and I wonder if I have finally struck something that lies beyond K@rine's ability to emulate. It might, of course, merely be that I haven't provided enough information on Xan, who was only fourteen or fifteen when her family moved from the small coastal settlement of Medina, where I had spent my entire life up until that point, to the major town of Beacon several hundreds of kilometres inland. It capped what, for me, had been a tumultuous year, and preceded a couple of utterly miserable ones. Xan had been, I suppose, my first – chaste – love, a realisation I came to at around the same time that I understood that I was in the wrong body...

'You may tell yourself that,' "Xan" says at last. 'But I suspect it was something you needed to do, just for yourself.'

Xan would not have said anything like that, I tell myself. *At least, not the Xan I knew, not the Xan I still carry around in my head. I don't know where you're getting this, K@rine...*

And, unbidden, a memory. Of what it feels like to awaken with an erection.

How nostalgic. How sad. How... awkward.

It's been tempting, to think back on Xan. Tempting, but ultimately hollow. It's the Now that I must concern myself with.

'Quit,' I say.

I'm now, within stellar-system terms, the slimmest iota of distance from the search volume proper, but still a daycycle away from bridging that gulf.

I continue to review contradictory pieces of information as they splash into the mind-pool. I explore, at second-hand, the spaces being trawled by the search fleet, in a real-time animation which *Peregrinator* has served up: the dart-shaped mil craft, the oblately globular DSSAR ships each with its attendant remora'd probes, the messily irregular forms of the salvage vessels. But if it shows anything, the simulation merely reveals that the *Bougainvillaea* has already run out of places to hide.

Such powerful, futile, arithmetic precision. But it's a simple doodle that finally does it. I'm sketching, on a flatchart, our present position and heading relative to Ashé, to Jotunheim, and to the assigned centre of the search volume. I have the chart mark out the timelines between these points – measures of the lightspeed signalling delay between any pair of points. And I notice something which, when I think about it, hits like a kick in the face.

Timelines. I have *Peregrinator* bring up the record of the timings for the *Bougainvillaea* distress call, received at lightspeed by the *Torosaurus*, by Ashé, by Ashé-L5, and by Utgard. Four widely-spaced receivers, each recording to a few microseconds the onset of the signal's arrival. I get *Peregrinator* to plot the appropriate locations for the receiving stations, for the epoch of the signal's interception. The vectors for the respective time delays, the time taken in each instance for the signal to reach the receiver, are of unknown absolute length, but their relative intervals are precisely defined: they give, together, a unique location for the *Bougainvillaea* at the time of the signal's broadcast, and that location is, indeed, at the centre of the volume of space within which the mil vessels, the salvage craft, and the DSSAR fleet are all searching. The geometry of the problem makes perfect sense.

And yet… I instruct *Peregrinator* to adjust one timing, just one, by a fraction of a second. And am disturbed at the result.

There is no redundancy in the timings.

K@rine hands collision-avoidance responsibility to the shipmind, and responds promptly to my page. 'Charmain?' it asks.

'I have a question.'

'Certainly. Does this relate to the Wlodek singleship's pursuit and imminent interception?'

'No. I have no idea what game Wlodek is playing. But it wouldn't surprise me to learn it's just a ruse to acquire an altflight-capable vessel, something concocted in haste when Peregrinator emerged so far off-target. This whole thing looks set to go belly-up, and Borken's going to take the flak. Wlodek might not want to stay in-system for that.'

'So… this is not your question?'

'No, it's worse. K@rine, what are the *Bougainvillaea*'s model class identifiers?'

'Propulsion and ship frame are Borken Three. Lifesystems and environmental engineering are Notocero Gamma. Charmain, these details are in the base-level public record.'

It's not the answer I'd been expecting; but then K@rine, as a semi-autonomous artificial intellect, is heavily equipped with error-filtering (read: homogenising) protocols, and is therefore perhaps not immune.

But there's maybe still a way. Not all of K@rine's stored knowledge is subjected to fact-checking, because not all of K@rine's "memories" are assumed to be objective. 'What if I ask "Miguel"?' I ask.

'What do you mean, "ask Miguel"?'

'Mig, what are the *Bougainvillaea*'s model class identifiers?'

'I don't know why you'd be asking me that, Char,' says K@rine, smoothly adopting Miguel's east-coast intonation. 'But far as I know, it's Borken Three, Notocero Delta.'

'Quit. K@rine, you note the discrepancy?'

'Yes. But I am at a loss to account for it.'

'I'm not. Somebody's muddied the mind-pool. K@rine, what are Notocero's affiliations at Eps Eri?'

'There are many. Notocero has business agreements with produce distributors, smart componentry fabricators, bespoke engineering firms, freighters, tachyonics, knowledge brokers, legal, synthetic-nutrition experts, mining…'

'Stick to the ones in which Notocero has, or could be construed to have, a controlling interest.'

It is still a fairly long list; though chiefly, I judge, small fry, with two or three exceptions. It's the latter of these exceptions which sets my teeth on edge. A Gliese-65-registered asteroid-mining concern, currently working the Jotunheim trojans.

The *Torosaurus*. The vessel that first reported detection of the *Bougainvillaea*'s shortlived radio signal. Which makes Creasey, the *Torosaurus*' captain, a Notocero employee, or near enough.

Now why would he not disclose that?

An awful thought strikes me. I need to review the guided tour that Creasey gifted upon my proxy.

Of them all – Antal, Gustav, Mohamed, all the others – the worst, by far, was Lucent. While with the others it was, mostly, just a game, with Lucent it was more. I remember beatings, kicks, ambushes. And though he was not a big youth – almost, I could doubt that he had yet embarked on the adolescence that was sweeping through the school's upper classes like a slow-spreading influenza – there was a viciousness about him, an appetite, a ruthlessness which quite eclipsed his physical shortcomings. I'd seen him take on larger targets than myself, and reduce them to quelled, bruised debasement, but it seemed as though once he grew aware of my ill-judged disclosure to Imogen, Lucent decided to focus on my torment.

It got so I dreaded free time, at school. In class there was a limit to humiliation's extent, for though there was a strong flavour of *persona non grata* about me, and though the teachers seemed invariably to share this judgmental attitude towards me, there were rules which constrained the behaviour of those who disapproved of me. Outside the classroom, in the maze of subtly curving subterranean passages that was our school, there were no such rules. Full of blind intersections and few escape routes, it was an excellent habitat for a bully.

Around the buttressed, enamel-walled, muralled corridors of the school grounds, I would seek quiet corners in which to hide; I attempted to sign up for extracurricular activities, such as the geo club or the miniature ekranoplaners, which would keep me within the comparative safety of organised groups. But often these clubs would not have me: I was tainted, not right according to The Way that held sway in our community. And even when I did succeed in taking sanctuary, for a lunchtime or a free period, Lucent would let me know that I had not escaped. He would contrive to walk past the dust-smeared windows, at frequent intervals, and to look in, casually skewering me with his stare. Or he would be waiting outside, fists bunched, when I emerged, sun-blinded, into the quadrangle's baking heat. The bruises he inflicted, deep, painful things, would still be there a week hence. At any time I might wear the decorations of four, five, six sessions of his assault. And each time he would smile toothily, or sneer to show me how much he enjoyed his mastery over me.

Lucent made my life a misery. One afternoon he yet again accosted me; in desperation, I leaned into him, kissed him on the lips, and told him that now he would burn in hell with me. He pushed me, arms thumping like pistons against my chest so that I stumbled and fell back. Pain sharp as a scalpel stabbed through my elbows a split second before my back and head thudded solidly onto the gravel. Then there were half a dozen vicious kicks, to my side – waist, thigh – and then, for good measure, he spat onto my face. His spittle tasted of ham and stale bread. He turned and wandered off, leaving me to my agony. It was several minutes before anyone crossed the hot, scrabblegrassed quadrangle to come and check on me, though there had been a few distant witnesses to the assault. It was, I think, the worst beating I had had – three cracked ribs, abrasions all along my arms, bruises below my right hip that took a couple of months to disappear – but it was also the last time Lucent Demetriodes ever used violence on me, or indeed acknowledged my existence in any way, other than to look past me with an expression of utter disgust. I guess I had, somehow, found his weak spot.

The pain was severe. But the body heals, over time. Doesn't it?

'They're dead. They're all dead.'

My proxy's comment, innocent of deeper intent, is on the flowers withering in a glass vase, which sits upon a large wooden table. But there's an almost-subliminal flash of panic in Creasey's response. And my face chills with the burgeoning suspicion of what has occurred.

*

64

I want this to be untrue, with more desperation than I have ever felt. But my intuition says otherwise.

'K@rine, we need to transmit a couple of messages. And I have no idea who we can trust.'

'Charmain, I do not know what to advise. But I have news I believe you will find unwelcome.'

I snort. 'Try me.'

'We have received a transmission from Borken—'

'Wlodek. Ignore him. We have other things to worry about.'

'It is not Wlodek, Charmain. The transmission originates from Borken HQ itself, Sol system. It checks out.'

'They sent an *altspace transmission*?'

'They shipped it. It arrived via the *Hellebore*, from Tau Ceti. I gather that, with current flight schedules, this was the quickest way for them to reach—'

'Yes, yes. This message. What does it tell us?'

'Charmain, the mission has been concluded.'

'*What?* Why?'

'It does not say. Beyond commenting that the search effort is best left to the resources stationed in-system.'

I load the message. The transmission idents certainly look credible. Worst, the message – which is moderately self-aware – has the audacity to commiserate with me for my loss.

My loss? How does Borken HQ know? How long has the ship's comms system been leaking details of my private life?

I kill the set of transmitted instructions, and turn to the android. 'We ignore this.'

'Charmain?' I don't believe I have ever heard K@rine sound so alarmed. 'But the transmission—'

'We ignore it,' I repeat.

'I will, of course, do as you instruct. But Charmain, the *Hellebore* has also forwarded the transmission to TransMig. We are no longer authorised to participate in the search. And the local authorities know this.'

'Then we'll need to move *quickly*.'

'Charmain, is this wise?'

'Wisdom went out the hatch a long time back.'

'Charmain?'

'Ignore it. Look, we need to send a message. Loud and wide.'

'While I believe that I have disabled the comms system's override, I cannot guarantee—'

'Understood. But I don't think that matters. I'm done keeping secrets.'

'Can I ask how this relates to our search for the *Bougain—*'

'The *Bougainvillaea*'s lost. It's not here. I don't think it ever was. K@rine, this isn't a search. This was *never* a search. It's a cover-up. Some of them know it, some of them don't. And I don't know who to trust.'

'But the data—'

'People *lie*, K@rine,' I say, my voice thick with ill-repressed feeling. 'I thought you'd know that by now.'

seven

'You really do have trust issues, don't you?'

We have ceased deceleration; thrust is now serving a different purpose.

Our heading is towards Groombridge 1618, and I have sent despatches to Ashé TransMig and to the *Victory Through Prudence*. These communications confirm that Borken has ceased active involvement in the search – they know as much anyway, it does me no harm to play along – and advise that, on company instructions, *Peregrinator* is preparing for altspace transit to the neighbouring star system. It is a less-than-completely-accurate statement of intent, which I am hoping will serve, for now.

Scratch the cover story, and you will find problems. Groombridge 1618 is an implausible destination: Borken has no interests there, no corporate presence, very little in the way of previous commercial involvement. Yet it *is* an inhabited settlement, with the virtue of lying close to the plane of Eps Eri's ecliptic, and happens to be within a few degrees of *Peregrinator*'s true target. I am hoping the Ashéan powers-that-be are more concerned with the assurance of my imminent exit from the local system than with the exact destination. As a cover story, it won't remain credible for more than a fraction of a daycycle, but it might be enough to put us beyond reach of mil pursuit for the duration of our voyage.

The hope that the Jotunheim trojans, the gas giant's trailing retinue of asteroids, may hold the key to the *Bougainvillaea's* disappearance has been a fleeting one. With the suspect signal-timing datum discounted, the resulting vector of possible locations for the lost liner lies well out of Eps Eri's ecliptic plane, intersecting only at the currently-scrutinised search volume. (Which leads me to suspect that the bogus timing has been chosen for this effect, leading as it does to the false expectation that the *Bougainvillaea* might have somehow been on an interplanetary trajectory, thereby discouraging more widely-flung searches for the vessel.) But if the asteroids cannot shed any light on the ship's fate, something – or someone – within the region has the answers I seek. The answers I dread.

Already the field of trojan asteroids stretches across the full span of ecliptic space ahead of us. Within this smear, the asteroids are as yet invisible at naked-eye resolution, apparent only under significant magnification; the gas giant in whose gravitational thrall they congregate is itself only the merest orb off to *Peregrinator's* port side. The dozens of mining vessels which prey on the more mineralogically alluring of the field's diverse space-rocks are also widely-scattered. It has taken some deep searching through the mind-pool to find the information I need. Though the identity and location of mining craft is publically accessible, it is not exactly *easily* accessible. The rock I want is JT 16135, a metal-rich crumb some fifty-five degrees astern of Jotunheim.

It will take us another three daycycles to reach JT 16135, and the *Torosaurus*, at which point I will need to decide what I do.

It's been a problem I've had this entire mission. You'd think I might be used to it by now.

'Of course, asteroids are always going to be more lucrative than comets. Scarcity of trace metals, difficulty in refining, and the indium thing, of course, which is paramount these days... by comparison, there's just no collateral in carbohydrates,' "Paolo" tells me. Which is typical – always, with him, the focus on the practical. He was never one to divulge of his innermost workings. This is, perhaps, what Nasreen saw in him – she always had more of a trace of the *sensible* about her than did I, and Paolo could give her that, and a ticket off Ashé; and, ultimately, a son.

'Why didn't it work out?' I say.

'But it *did* work out,' replies "Paolo". 'You think fifteen years is not working out?'

'I'd be interested to hear Ahmed's opinion on that,' I counter.

'Ah, but Ahmed's not here, is he?'

'Quit,' I say, more sharply than intended. 'K@rine, that was below the belt. And you know it.'

We have attracted pursuit. The "Wlodek" singleship has, unsurprisingly, adjusted course in tandem with our own manoeuvre. And the *Catechism* and the *Small But Mighty* have broken off their search activities and have commenced acceleration on a course to intercept *Peregrinator*.

Its true nature revealed, "Wlodek" has not attempted any new communications for the past couple of daycycles, and I am left wondering at both its original motivation and its current intent. But the singleship is gaining, and stands to catch us within the next daycycle or so. Even if it does not, the act of braking to a rendezvous with the Jotunheim trojans will leave *Peregrinator* a sitting duck, vulnerable to what is, in effect, a self-directed and high-tech kinetic energy weapon. And though my vessel is ex-mil, it is of course unarmed.

Of the other vessels in pursuit, the *Catechism*, a destroyer, cannot plausibly overtake us before it is too late; the cruiser *Small But Mighty* has, I judge, the capability to intercept, but does not appear to be piling on the double-figure g forces that would be necessitated. I am not sure whether to view this as a positive or a negative.

Our legitimate presence at Eps Eri has expired. The powers-that-be know this. The question is: what can I salvage, from the remainder of my time here?

It is the work of a few hours for K@rine and me to prepare the proxy, and to send it to the one person in a position of authority whom I feel I can trust. It will, of course, be detected by the mil craft behind us, and possibly by the "Wlodek" singleship also. The proxy's intent is simple, and limited: it is to ask Miguel, at the Bureau of Information, to tightbeam a transmission of gratitude to Anders Wlodek – the *real* Anders Wlodek, whom I strongly believe to have remained in the vicinity of Utgard during this whole escapade – for his assistance during *Peregrinator*'s mission at Eps Eri. I cannot directly report my suspicions to the Ashéan mil vessels: Wlodek is an indentured resident of this system, while I am rapidly becoming an overstayer, so there is no reason to believe that the military would pay any heed to my assertions of the real Wlodek's whereabouts, nor to the nature of the singleship's occupant. Nor do I think it probable that a transmission from *Peregrinator*, direct to Utgard, would be received by Wlodek himself, or paid any credence by anyone in a position of authority. Such actions on my part would only achieve the outcome of alerting Ashé to my own current deception. In reaching out to Miguel, I am hoping the BoI's resources can pinpoint Wlodek's true location and can message him without arousing his initial suspicions.

Will the mil craft make the connection that they are sharing a heading with an unmanned singleship – an undeclared missile – approaching the Jotunheim trojans, a territory of considerable value to the Ashéan economy?

Two hours pass. I make a modest course correction, which is soon echoed by the singleship. But it is the response of the mil ships, the *Small But Mighty* and the *Catechism*, which is more disconcerting. They commence hard acceleration. And then they vanish.

Stealth mode. War footing.

I report altspace drive problems, and request assistance from the cloaked mil ships currently in pursuit. It's the best I can do, the best I can think of.

We have been steadily decelerating for the best part of a daycycle, and have spilled over ninety percent of our velocity, while the singleship slips ever closer. I try to guess at Wlodek's motives: he wants *Peregrinator* intact, still, I am sure of it, but if he fears I have stumbled onto the secret of the *Bougainvillaea*, he may decide otherwise. (But I must also remember that the singleship's pilot is not Wlodek, but a hastily-assembled proxy: its responses are not going to be those of a genuine human being. Will it err towards circumspection, or to ruthlessness?)

I have watched the singleship's distance diminish steadily… alarmingly. It is only forty thousand kilometres behind now, and gaining on *Peregrinator* at almost a thousand kilometres a minute. Thirty-five thousand kilometres. Thirty thousand. Twenty-seven thousand.

Finally, I see the flare of a braking burn. *Rendezvous?* From such a mismatched set of velocities? Does the proxy still somehow believe that I can be coerced into giving up *Peregrinator*, for delivery to Wlodek?

But the braking burn blooms, and then dies, after just a few seconds. I feel a chill at my back, knowing that – whether by railgun or by gamma-ray laser or by tactical AM missile – I have just witnessed the death of a spaceship. The knowledge that there was nothing alive on the singleship does little to mitigate the shock, or to soothe. If the stealthed ships of the Ashéan military have decided to escalate matters to this extent…

Seconds elapse. Then minutes. My heartbeat ebbs away from a panicked, helpless crescendo. If I am in their sights, they are holding fire, for now. A half-hour passes, and the singleship's still-warm debris cloud hurtles past, its fragments mostly too small and too distant to pose any threat beyond "object lesson". There is one reasonably solid thump, as something impacts the nosecone, but it cannot be more than about fifty grams. Eps Eri herself has flung far worse at us, over the past several daycycles.

Somewhere, most probably on Utgard, the flesh and blood Wlodek has noted the singleship's destruction. I can almost feel sorry for him. Until I remind myself that *Peregrinator* has never been more than a getaway vehicle for him, a method of fleeing Eps Eri.

Wlodek is done, as a threat. I hope.

Now for Creasey. Assuming I am allowed the opportunity.

I am acutely conscious of my visibility, my vulnerability. I find myself wishing that *Peregrinator* retained its own stealth capability. But the more rational side of me knows such an act would provoke a mil response which, for the moment, is in abeyance. My entire strategy now depends on holding plainly to one precise trajectory.

"Object lesson", here I come...

With less than three hundred thousand kilometres to go, *Peregrinator*'s drive gutters, in what I hope is a passable imitation of an exhaustion of fuel. A few apparently-futile attempts to manoeuvre using the attitude rockets leave us barreling nose-forward on a direct collision course towards the *Torosaurus*, at twenty-nine kilometres per second. Will this action mislead the mil vessels? Perhaps, though I doubt it. Will it pass a board of inquiry? Most certainly not. Will it provide something for Creasey, captain of the *Torosaurus*, to think about?

I sincerely hope so.

Even at one hundred thousand kilometres per hour, a light-second takes three hours to traverse. It's an uncomfortably long time in which to reappraise the wisdom of my plan, to question how long the mil craft will hold their fire, and to wonder just what will happen if Creasey does not respond as I hope. "Messy" would not even begin to describe it.

The transport lounge in Minke was bustling, and sharp with late-autumn chill. It was hard to imagine my sister, a daughter of desert heat, making her home in this city, on this world: yet here she was.

I passed Ahmed back to her. 'He's gorgeous,' I said, eventually. Any other expression seemed inadequate.

She beamed, blushed. Rearranged the coverlet over Ahmed's sleeping form, only his small, perfectly-formed face showing past the shawl's hem.

'He has his aunt's eyes,' Paolo said. The words, though welcome – and Paolo had always managed to sound accepting – seemed odd, foreign. I had long ago taken ownership of the word "woman"; this "aunt" business was still new to me.

'He has the Miyaki chin,' I replied, 'for which he may yet come to curse you both. But he has his father's nose, and that has to be a good thing.'

Ahmed stirred in his sleep, wrinkled his face, smiled at one of those private jokes known only to babies, and blew a half-hearted bubble of saliva.

'Thank you for coming, Sister,' Nasreen told me, adjusting the shawl yet again.

'How could I stay away?' I asked. I chose not to elaborate on how much of my salary and my leave allowance had been spent on taking a passenger berth from Sol to Tau Ceti, for this. 'You'll take him to meet Mama?'

Nasreen's brow furrowed. 'Eventually. It's not so—'

'Don't leave it too long,' I admonished. 'The last I heard, she was… and you know how much the sight of her grandchild would mean to her.'

'I've sent pictures,' she said. 'Not the same, I know.'

I spent ten days, in total, with Nasreen and Paolo and Ahmed: the ship's schedule did not permit longer. We parted, lumps in throats, with a promise to meet again in a few years at most, so I could see my nephew as a boy, not just a baby. It was a promise that, in that time, in that place, was not difficult to make.

But you know what they say. That there is a last time for everything.

I hold course, hurtling towards the *Torosaurus*. After many minutes it becomes apparent that my aim is not quite perfect. *Peregrinator* is forced to make a subtle attitude-rocket burn to nudge us onto a more exact ballistic intercept. Still the mining ship takes no action, though as it morphs from pinprick to oblong shape in our forward viewscreens, Creasey's defensive opportunities diminish while his offensive choices multiply. The miner may not be armed, as such, but it possesses a good deal of plant designed with the specific purpose of deconstructing solid matter, and presumably is also equipped with a complement of anti-collision missiles and rammers. (Vessels this large aren't accustomed to dodge; they shunt aside.) I cannot believe that Creasey has not yet thrown anything at us, whether rock, rocket, or plasma exhaust. I am almost certain I would, if the roles were reversed. Surely, he must take some action against us – is he perhaps waiting until we are too close to escape his response? And yet such a delay would seem suicidal, on his part…

Unless Creasey feels that his nose must be kept clean in whatever follows, so as to avoid scrutiny of whatever has already transpired.

My resolve wobbles. But, in the end, Creasey blinks first. With the distance between ships down to about ten thousand kilometres, *Torosaurus* lumbers its way out of our flight path. She is running heavy. (*But how heavy?*)

I record the manoeuvre in full, at maximum magnification, and transmit the data towards our mil pursuers. And to anyone else listening. Then, while we hurtle past the miner at a velocity frightening to contemplate, I commence reorientation of *Peregrinator* for decel.

The mining ship is massive; and while in active asteroid-harvesting mode (as it is now), it will be additionally encumbered and a brutish thing to manoeuvre, especially if damage to the deployed mining equipment is to be averted. It will take considerable time for *Peregrinator* to brake, but it may well take Creasey longer to bring his vessel under full control.

For what I'm putting *Peregrinator* through, Borken will have my hide. Her engines are only safety-rated to an absolute maximum of nine point two *g*. But the impact-gel-filled crash case in which I'm currently cocooned is rated to eleven, so I figure…

But there is a problem. The altspace transmitter and the main lightspeed transmit dish both fail in the minutes-long impact that is our punishing braking burn. We are not dead in the water, but we cannot talk to anyone.

And, in orchestrating the manoeuvre that I hope will convince the *Small But Mighty*'s commanding officer of the *Torosaurus*' deception, I may well have come sufficiently close to committing an actively hostile act that *Peregrinator* is now viewed as a combatant. Certainly, we have not made the exit from the system which we were claiming…

My every instinct, echoed by a heart still hammering from such a brutal decel profile, tells me otherwise; but it may well be that the safest place for me, right now, is aboard the *Torosaurus*.

eight

Isn't this the whole purpose of having a lions' den?

The *Torosaurus* is a specialised asteroid-mining platform licensed out of Gliese 65 to Elmeraite Resources. For the past two weeks, it has been operating on contract to Beltmetals AV, an Ashé-based minerals consortium. And both Elmeraite and Beltmetals are bodies in which Notocero has a less-than-obvious, but undeniable, controlling interest.

It's a big ship, for a crew of one.

Size estimation across a vacuum is always tricky. But the *Torosaurus* looks to be as large as an altspace-capable ship can get within the limits of CAD technology. Straight-edged, bulky, unremittingly utilitarian, she is a brick of a thing. A *weathered* brick. There is no cockpit visible, no navigation or obs blister, no porthole. Streaks, scrapes and innumerable small dents decorate her bare-metal panelling. Adjoining panels misalign in a few spots. The ship's ident logo, displayed on multiple facets, is part-obliterated in one place by a disconcertingly prominent (and probably years-old) impact puncture, while on another face the auxiliary transmission coil shows extensive damage. Still, her running lights are alive, and I have no reasons to believe that her recent evasive sidestep has diminished her capabilities in any way.

Suited up aboard *Peregrinator*'s shuttle, I feel as though I'm pinned at the centre of a primitive neon sign, with the hazard illumination patterned in the universally-accepted signal for "mayday". I doubt that the signalling will fool the *Torosaurus*' captain for even an instant, but it may give him pause against taking provocative or retaliatory action, particularly in view of the approaching military attention.

I feign uncertainty as to the location of the mining ship's docking collar, the better to make a wide surveillance circuit around the *Torosaurus*. (And indeed, since the vessel does not spin, my pretend confusion is quite plausible.) The mining vessel's underbelly has JT 16135 pinioned to it: a small planetesimal, no more, I judge, than fifty metres on its long axis. It makes for an incongruous juxtaposition of the primeval and the manufactured, like a bloated mechanical spider feeding on a web-entombed insect. Several squat, boxy machines manoeuvre around the captive asteroid, inflicting precise, judicious damage upon it. It's not apparent, on a first inspection, if this represents business-as-usual or if the *Torosaurus* is checking for damage to her cargo / prey item in the aftermath of her recent motion. The machines moving around the asteroid are overseen by one presumably-suited human – Creasey?

I instruct K@rine to bring the shuttle in slowly, though my instinct calls for haste. This is a pure play-for-time – though I do not feel entirely secure in the matter of the mil ships' intentions, I am banking that Creasey is similarly less-than-certain, and hoping that he will, I hope, hold any fire while I am outside the ship and (perhaps) in the *Small But Mighty*'s view.

It is the logical approach. But logic does not quiet the heart.

The *Torosaurus'* docking collar does not respond to my hail. I check my suit's seals – *an old pilot is a cautious pilot* – and make my way to the shuttle's lock. This may well be fruitless: Creasey can very easily disable external controls for the mining craft's docking collar and airlocks. Although, if the suited figure I saw was indeed Creasey, it would be reasonable to expect some degree of external control to remain active.

K@rine has brought us in close, and the *Torosaurus* is not rotating in any direction: the spacewalk is as straightforward as they come and lasts less than a half-minute, though for every one of those seconds I am acutely conscious of my physical vulnerability, just the layers of the suit to protect me from not only the natural hazards of the environment, but other artificial dangers as well. It is only after I depress the control patch beside the docking collar's auxiliary airlock that I wonder, belatedly, what countermeasures Creasey might have in place.

The airlock's outer hatch slashes open without incident. I move carefully through the opening; the hull seals behind me, and the lock's inner hatch opens in turn. The chamber revealed within is die-straight, cylindrical, clinical in its featurelessness, and leading apparently fifty metres or more directly into the innards of the voluminous mining ship. Save for the green-suited figure waiting within, anchored via a glove-hold to a wall bracket halfway down the cylindrical corridor's length, it is so empty as to remind me of the barrel of a projectile weapon. But the connection my mind now chooses to make, and hold to, is with the subterranean passageways of my school.

Creasey, whoever he might be, is not Lucent Demetriodes. I must remember this. The past is not the present.

The hatch closes behind me. My head is muzzy, my extremities are still tingling with the blood-disorientation that weightlessness brings following a period of high *g*. If I am suddenly stricken with renewed thoughts of *this is not at all a good idea…* these now, I presume, would fall under the subhead of "too late for that, Charmain".

The figure in the green suit stays motionless until I draw close. It is not Creasey, is not in fact human, but a metallic and muscled android, with more than a nod to the curvature of the generic female form.

The discomfort I'm feeling is expected, but I wish, at least, that my gloved hands would stop shaking.

Several corridors later, gravity is at normal strength. Notwithstanding, I'm disoriented on several levels. At first, it's my inability to fathom the eerie sense of *déjà vu* that I feel, until I recollect that, in a sense, I *have* been here before, by proxy. I've seen these passageways through the eyes of my simulation. And yet there seem to be differences in the layout of the vessel, with several sections blocked off. The "lounge", for example, which was a focal point of the proxy's tour of the ship, appears no longer to be accessible. Just what is Creasey hiding?

To add to my disorientation, I'm still at a loss to work out how the *Torosaurus*, which is not under any overall rotation, manages to adopt the unmistakable signature – coriolis and curved "flat" flooring – of spin-grav. But other concerns are more pressing.

The green-suited android that, since my arrival in the airlock, has functioned as my captor releases its grip on my shoulder. It (she) has directed me to the entrance of a cubic chamber (not part of the proxy's experience of the vessel) that appears to have no other exits, although the wall and ceiling decorations – a subtly-animated terrestrial rainforest vista, in wraparound mural – may mask portals. Though the walls are a distraction, the hullmetal-floored room is dominated by an incongruous and heavy-framed wooden table. There is, I estimate, room to seat eight around the table, but only one chair exists: a flight chair, gimballed and presumably bolted to the floor. The chair's occupant, seated directly across from me, is eating.

Creasey is, in some respects, an anticlimax, almost I would say a disappointment. He's a short man, a little tubby, pale almost to the suggestion of the old-style Caucasian complexion, or of anaemia; the lack of dermal pigmentation offset, heightened, by the blackness of his thinning hair. His cheeks and chin are scraggly: he has not taken the time to depilate within the past several daycycles. He is dressed in nondescript grey overalls: they look worn but clean. He has not even looked up at our arrival, but busies himself with the messy task of consuming the sticky ribs, beans and rice on the plate in front of him. A fork exists for the vegetable matter (which looks, to my eye, quite finely structured – perhaps the *Torosaurus* has a hydroponics suite?), but he eats the ribs with his fingers, places the short strips of bone on one side of the plate.

Beans and rice are standard ship fare: easily synthesised, almost as straightforwardly grown for those who distrust synthfood. But galley systems that synthesise bone inclusions, in meat substrates, are expensive and inefficient. Something to do with the difficulty in handling high concentrations of calciferous precursor agents in matter recycling networks. I would not expect to find such a system in a single-occupant mining vessel, nor does Creasey strike me as the gourmet type.

The android nudges me, with a firm quick pressure in the small of my back, towards the table. I stumble, balance thrown off by the unfamiliar spin-grav, and put my hands out to grip the table's edge, directly across from Creasey. He continues eating. I strive to put as much weight as possible on my hands; my shins ache as an aftermath of the crash-decel of *Peregrinator*'s braking burn. The android is stationed behind me, so close I can feel, through the skin of my own suit, the press of its hips against my back. It is not confining me, exactly. But I am not in doubt that it can move more quickly, and with much greater violence, than I can currently muster.

I relinquish my grip on the table-edge for a brief interval, during which I crack my neck-seal, shuck my helmet, and fasten it to the quick-release bracket at my hip. Then I continue to stand for several minutes. Around me and Creasey, the simulated wildlife of the rainforest vista scampers, calls, hides, and hunts. I watch a monkey of some sort – long-tailed, long-limbed, high-contrast monochrome – attempt an audacious tree-to-tree leap, miscalculate, and fall, screeching, to what would seem to be its death.

The air within the chamber does not feel fresh.

Eventually, Creasey pushes his mostly-finished meal to one side, wipes the grease and sauce from his lips and fingers with a brocade napkin, and looks up.

My eyes meet his. There is no warmth there, on either side. I wait to see if he will speak; he does not. I wonder, idly, how long it will take him to decide I will not first break the impasse.

From some alcove camouflaged by the rainforest diorama, a second android – identical in appearance, it seems, to the one at my back – appears, smoothly gathers up the remnants of Creasey's meal, wipes clean the tabletop, and leaves. The silence is ruptured.

'In the context,' Creasey begins, 'the words "this *is* a surprise" would have to be something of an understatement.'

I don't hurry my reply. I hold his stare for as long as I dare – remembering that this man will in all probability kill me, to save himself; but knowing that he will want to know what I know, and what I have told others, before he does so. I remind myself that I have faced down demons before this.

I take fifteen seconds before I speak. Then six small words. 'My sister was on that ship.'

'Which ship was that?' he asks.

'The *Bougainvillaea*,' I say, with more force than I'd wish. My shins burn with fatigue.

'Yes. Tragic. But I don't see how that gives you leave to – let's not make any bones – launch an unprovoked attack on an innocent mining vessel. I do hope Borken – it *was* Borken, wasn't it? – is going to be forthcoming with an apology. As well as reparations for the structural damage sustained through hastily-implemented evasive manoeuvres.'

'I'm only sorry you dodged, Creasey,' I reply. 'Not that it'll help you.'

'Ms Mertz,' says Creasey. 'You seem to be misreading the situation, probably through your grief. Understandable, but I really don't see what you're implying.'

'I think you do. You've been lying for *weeks*, Creasey, about what happened to the *Bougainvillaea*.'

'Please. You launch some kind of kamikaze assault on my vessel, you as good as *break your way aboard*, and now you see fit to cast god-only-knows what manner of aspersions about… well, I'm really not sure what. Frankly, it's offensive. And I have better things to be doing with my time.'

'Then give me what I came for, and let me go.'

'Let you go? Ms Mertz, you're the one who chose to board. You're not being held against your will.'

And I could. I could turn, step past this android, and move back through the ship to the airlock. But I don't have what I've come for, and that's *knowledge*. Closure. A confession. My debt, in the circumstances, to my sister.

'You would, of course, have to wait until your shuttle powers up again,' says Creasey. 'I found it necessary to to deactivate its systems when I had it brought in for docking. It might take a couple of hours for full operational status to be restored. Longer, perhaps, for your android.'

K@rine. I'm not sure why his assertion fills me with something more than dread, but evidently it shows. Creasey smiles. Not a pretty sight.

'Ms Mertz,' he says, rising from his chair. Standing, he is still shorter than I, though the machine behind me overtops us both. 'Perhaps you'd like to tell me why you're here. Or perhaps you could start by informing me of who else you've shared your delusions with.'

'The *Small But Mighty*, for starters,' I say. 'And the *Catechism*.'

'Oh, I don't think so. Because – and let me see if I can follow your twisted reasoning here – *if* you felt convinced that I had in some way been involved in misdoing, *and* you had firm evidence of this, you might then logically have passed this information on to the mil authorities. But that being the case, you would not have raced to get here ahead of the *Small But Mighty*, and you would not then have forced your way on board my vessel, placing yourself in what would have to be, in your mind, unnecessary danger.'

Creasey makes his way slowly around the table, until he is standing little more than a metre from me, off to one side. There is a musky scent which catches in my nose. It must have been a month or more since I have smelt another's body odour, and Creasey's is rank. It is a strong smell, sour, disturbing.

I bite my lip, and try to turn my body to face Creasey. But his bulky feminised android pinions my vac-suited arms to my side, and I am forced instead to keep my head turned towards the miner. The machine's grip is firm, precise, not painful, but I do not doubt that it could inflict agony, if it so chose. If it was so directed. This message sent, it releases me again.

I tell myself I know something he does not, and hope it is true. I force myself to smile at Creasey, a slow and deliberate smile.

He does not smile back. Instead, Creasey glances away at something I cannot discern – some feature of the forest diorama, perhaps? – before returning his gaze to me. 'No, the only rationale I can see for your course of actions is that you have not informed the mil authorities, do *not* in fact have any firm evidence for this… fantasy to which you allude, and perhaps are in fact no longer authorised to operate within Ashé local space – in which case what you're attempting here is a gamble, a race against time, an attempt to convince me to confess, or something similar. For something which, as I've already indicated, I didn't do.'

'You're wrong about something,' I begin, flinching as the android again reacts against my instinctive attempt to twist towards Creasey. 'I didn't race to get here before the *Small But Mighty*. I tried to ram you—'

'Yes. And thank you for your frank admission, which I'll be delighted to advertise on your behalf. My android has, of course, been recording this. But while we're exchanging hypotheticals, tell me what you think of this one. Your ship decelerates in extreme haste so as to – let's be polite – "rendezvous" with mine, and in the process you sustain major internal injuries for which I am able to offer you medical assistance. Sadly, shortly after you come aboard, you succumb to your injuries, which as the subsequent autopsy will confirm are indeed consistent with g-force-induced organ rupture.' He offers me a small, entirely cold, smile. 'This is a mining ship, Ms Mertz. And a very well-equipped one at that. I think you'd be surprised at how... dangerous... our centrifuges can be.'

'Are you threatening me, Creasey?'

'Threaten? No, Mertz. I would say you're the only one who has done that. On the contrary, I am merely warning you. A mining ship can be a hazardous vessel. For those who are not familiar with its pitfalls.'

The android's sudden grip is fierce, and I grunt in shock. There will be bruises beneath these sleeves. My hands begin to tingle as the circulation in my forearms is restricted. And then, once again, I am released, though still undeniably captive. Now that Creasey has resorted to open intimidation, now that he – perhaps – has a sense for where I am heading, he will not simply let me go.

'Maybe this is a gamble, like you said,' I concede, through teeth grimly gritted. 'I'm gambling here that your greed has caused your downfall.'

'Oh, you really are quite the dark horse, aren't you, Mertz? You *still* seem to think you've got something on me. Let me tell you what

nine

This might just have been a mistake.

Though they were obligated to offer the procedure, the medcentre surgeons made no secret of their disapproval. I was shown into a private room, one chair, no other furniture, no windows, and made to wait with no explanation while from the corridor I could hear the sounds of hospital activity. After what seemed a couple of hours I was visited by the surgeon, who explained in detail to me what would be done on the operating bench. It was detail I didn't need at that point, detail with which I was already familiar from earlier consultations. Just like the waiting, like the second "pre-operation" room I was subsequently shown into (with the posters and the interactive vids), the purpose seemed to be to demoralise, to confront, to offer one last chance to repent.

There were yet further delays, once I was shown into theatre and shaved and readied for surgery. They asked if I wished to speak to a Spiritual Welfare Officer, or to a family member. They asked if I would allow a cadre of med students to witness the operation. I declined, and felt a ramping, impotent fury. And a dread.

I had been anticipating this event for years. Awaiting the day, often with impatience. Now I had new doubts, and went awkwardly into the anaesthetic's embrace.

It was when I awoke after that first procedure, groggy, drugged almost to painlessness, that I decided I must leave Ashé. All through the latter years of schooling, through the social frustrations and ongoing humiliation of college, I had been determined to stick it out, to make "them" see. But surgery… the ominous acts of trust, the finality of the knife, and, yes, the numbing drugs… my mind was changed.

The urge to leave: it was an ill-formed thought, at first. But it kindled, it took hold while further surgery completed my alteration over the next days. By the time I had walked unaided down the corridors of Medina's residential section to my home room, on legs which might have been borrowed from Andersen's mermaid, I knew I could not let myself be bound by Eps Eri's leaden pull. I did not belong here. I was now not the person I had been, in their eyes. In my eyes? That was something I would yet figure out for myself.

Where would I go? I did not know. But I would walk free.

Escape. When you can, when nothing else has helped, escape.

It's not always an option.

I have seen centrifuges before. The centrifuges of deep-space mining vessels are large-capacity, overengineered drums designed to withstand the rigours of a high spin rate with an intrinsically heavy and irregular load, and the *Torosaurus*'s centrifuge is all of that. And yet—

I have accompanied the miner and his menacingly voluptuous android back to the axial shaft by which I first entered the *Torosaurus*. A smooth panel at the inward end of this corridor, removed by the android, has revealed a short extension to the main shaft, finished in some workaday grey alloy rather than the clean whiteness of the main passageway. Creasey, effortlessly at home in the weightlessness that persists along the axis, passes through into the grey zone. I am directed to follow. I have no time to think of physically confronting Creasey during the brief instant before the android manipulates its way in after us. In any case, my own zero-gee reflexes are poor and awkward; even without the android's proximity, I would be no match for Creasey in this environment.

There is an instrument cluster on the wall – or floor – or cylindrical surface – of this zone. We have been drifting away from it; or rather, I tell myself, it has been slowly rotating with the shaft's wall, away from our position. Creasey has half-jumped, half-glided across to the bank of instruments, has cushioned himself before activating a couple of the controls, and the cylinder wall's rotation has slowly and smoothly come to a halt. (At least, I have presumed that the rotation has ceased. I do not fully trust the evidence of my eyes, nor my stomach, and my inner ears do not, for the moment, know what to think.)

Another flat panel, in the opposite end of the cylinder – thus, pointing further in towards the belly of the immense ship – slides aside. This, now, brings up my first view of the centrifuge, coaxial with the corridors through which we have travelled to reach it. We have emerged into a protective cage which sits just in front of the centrifuge's maw (or just above it, depending on one's choice of perspective). A gate in the cage's side, which would give access to the 'fuge itself, is currently closed.

The drum of the centrifuge – which, as I watch, I can perceive to be slowly spinning, just a couple of revolutions per minute – is deep, and more than ten metres in diameter. It's a scale that dwarfs the machine's occupant: another of Creasey's androids, working at the rim of the centrifuge, is methodically bolting the back of a crash-couch to the concave side of the drum.

The pockmarks and grooves of the drum's working surface – the cylindrical cuff against which its load is pressed, tumbled, and buffeted during high rotation – are etched out in a pattern of smeared and stretched rust-marks, or of something that looks like rust, perhaps darker.

A queasy feeling strikes at my stomach.

Creasey unfastens the cage's gate, pushes me through the opening. There's an instant – and I see it – when I could take action. Not escape, no. But at least *delay*. By grabbing the gate's lip, I could swing myself back towards the cage, make some attempt to evade recapture.

I let it pass, and brace. Then I ricochet awkwardly from the drum's side. The guardian android from the cage has followed me in, and quickly has me caught, shackled, cuffed, towed to the waiting crash-couch.

Now alone in the cage, Creasey looks at last relaxed, no longer on edge. 'Eight g should do it, I think,' he says, in the conversational tone one might employ for the climate, or for an uncontroversial offering of entertainment.

'I hit eleven on the decel,' I retort, determined not to appear cowed while the android straps my boot-sheathed ankles to the couch's footrest. (And all the while, my heart hammering, my palms clammy, my legs quaking…)

'Perhaps,' says Creasey, still in the same offhand manner. 'But I can still smell the impact gel on you. You'll get none of that here. Eight will be plenty.'

We've reached the crux. Like a nurse, the android gently folds me forward at the hips, then bends my knees so I am forced to sit. It tethers my torso against the couch's padded back. The miner is right: although the couch is comfortable enough in this fractional-g environment, at eight g all the padding will become irrelevant. My own bones, my very organs, will crush me. And the centrifuge must be capable, if Creasey puts his mind to it, of reducing me to a lumpy jelly, or a paste. Those rust-marks at my feet didn't make themselves...

But there is one thing he does not yet know. 'Creasey,' I say, while the androids work together behind me, presumably checking the bolts that anchor the couch to the drum.

Amusement. 'Yes?'

I must angle my head up to meet Creasey's stare. I strive to appear calm, to convey a sense of self-control I cannot feel. 'I wasn't looking to ram you. I was looking to *weigh* you. Because you've been greedy.'

'Weigh me?' Serious now. Sharp.

Which means I must be careful, in how I place my words. And quick, probably. I lick my lips, bid my heart to quiet. 'The *Bougainvillaea*'s lost. I'm guessing something went catastrophically wrong with the Notocero lifesystems, something so wrong that you had to conceal it, ensure no-one would ever find it. In the absence of evidence, the blame would fall on Borken's drivesystem. But that only worked if it *stayed* lost, forever. Hence the timing trick.'

'Go on,' says Creasey, his voice slow, cold.

I breathe deep. 'But that still left a problem. The *Bougainvillaea* becomes a massive piece of incriminatory evidence, waiting to be uncovered at some indefinite point in the future. But it's also several hundred thousand tonnes of valuable metals and minerals. And you're in possession of a state-of-the-art mining platform, big enough to swallow a small asteroid whole. Easily big enough to ingest the *Bougainvillaea*, and to process it at your leisure.'

'I have never…' Creasey replies slowly, 'been subjected to such a – a monstrous accusation. If you are implying that I – that…' He exhales deeply, collects himself. 'You have a truly disturbed mind, Ms Mertz.' There is a careful anger behind his words. But behind *that*, his face blooms in flush.

'Raw materials. The good company man, the miner in you, wouldn't have let that opportunity go to waste.'

'That is a despicable suggestion, Mertz.' It looks as though he's using every one of his facial muscles to keep his expression unchanged.

'But not a lie,' I counter. I flinch, waiting for retribution. For the flick of a switch. 'It's over, Creasey.'

'How so? You're hardly going to walk out of this.'

'Perhaps not. But don't think that that will save you. I've had plenty of practice in guarding my own back, over the years.'

He forces a smile. 'Those instincts would appear to have let you down.'

'You think so? Killing me won't solve your problems. It'll only make them worse. That manoeuvre you pulled just now, to avoid collision with *Peregrinator*, will have been picked up by mil craft capable of detecting a sub-second attitude-jet burn at ten light-minutes' distance. They're going to have no trouble at all finding out the *Torosaurus* is more sluggish than it should be. Heavier. Full of material that isn't listed on the manifest. And just in case they miss it somehow, I've beamed it back to TransMig, and every planetary agency on Ashé I could think of. *Someone* will make you for the greedy, incautious, murderous creep that you are.'

Creasey doesn't reply. Judging by the expression on his face, he doesn't need to. And I know, as sure as I now know I will never see my sister again, that Creasey has just realised his mistake. The *little* mistake, that is, the one that points back to the gross, the unforgivable, the totally obscene error of judgment on his part, from a few weeks back. The error in his thinking that led him to treat an entire, dead, ship as *feedstock*. Rather than to report it.

So much raw material. Processed, compacted, there'd be plenty of places to conceal it all within the cavernous interior of a mining vessel. But it's still *mass*. And in a system as tightly regulated as Eps Eri, where a miner must specify each asteroid harvested, and the quantity of material gleaned from each, the added heft that had once been the *Bougainvillaea* would have made the *Torosaurus* measurably more sluggish, in the circumstance that it would find itself needing to take evasive action.

I'd captured the *Torosaurus*' burn in high-definition, wide-spectrum detail. And I'd beamed this back to the mil ships behind us, with the message *weigh it… weigh it… weigh it…*

'I got there too late,' Creasey admits, visibly struggling with the enormity of the secret he's held for the past few weeks. 'Two, three days by the time I found them.' Some shade of humanity finally animates his face. It's not pretty. 'It… like you said, the lifesystem. The big boys, the Notocero table-sitters, they'd had a hunch it could've done that. But they'd been convinced it'd never happen in real life. It happened.'

'*What* happened?' I prompt.

He shakes his head. 'Dead. Just dead. No propulsion, no comms, no environment conditioning. The whole stinking ship, near enough. Forty-three thousand people.'

It's grown suddenly cold in my suit. Something congeals in my chest. 'What do you mean, *near enough*?'

'What else was I to do?' Creasey asks, pointedly not meeting my stare. 'Forty-three thousand corpses, we couldn't let that come out. Not at any cost.'

The androids, their tasks in the centrifuge drum finished, move back towards Creasey's cage. I feel the rising rim of dread. If there is something else to say, something which will sway his mind, I must say it now.

But there is nothing. Nothing I can find, to cut through the awful static that fills my head.

We couldn't let that come out.

His confession made, Creasey presses a switch. And then, in some haste, he leaves the chamber, followed by his android guardians.

Coward.

Cursing, crying, I struggle, striving to extricate at least one arm. But the tethers are tight.

The 'fuge takes its time, is gentle to begin with. But all subtlety has faded after the first thirty seconds. Gravity, or something akin, swoops in, slings me backwards against the couch and presses hard, unrelenting. Each breath grows more difficult, more edged with pain as the weight of my ribcage increases. The suit's neck-flange presses against the back of my neck, the base of my skull. I unclench my fists, white-knuckle grip the couch's armrests with hands grown lead-heavy, grit my teeth, await the end. As the centrifuge picks up the pace, as I feel my world blur and narrow around me, I see an explosion blossom silently, angrily red in the direction of the corridor outside. Then darkness.

ten

'I have the Coriolis headache to end them all. K@rine, I really don't see what's so bad about having been deactivated.'

Dizzy beyond belief, my eyes refusing to focus, I am only dimly aware of the mil corpswoman who clasps an oxymask around my face and then commences to unstrap me. I try to smile at her, in show of gratitude for my rescue. But I cannot.

Nasreen is gone, and Ahmed, and Jian, and forty-three thousand others. I could never save them, and that will haunt me forever after. But I have brought down the sick creep who found them, and who then thought to conceal it. And, by so doing, to profit from it.

Raw materials.

I will ultimately, I suspect, express thanks that the *Small But Mighty* had seen fit to press the pace. But that, I think, must wait for another day.

Oblivion. Oblivion is good, for now.

It's done. Under mil arrest, Creasey confesses to the destruction of the *Bougainvillaea*.

Five vessels, the *Torosaurus* among them, had been sent secretly by Notocero to attempt to find the *Bougainvillaea* and to effect a rescue. But with the passenger craft dumped out of altspace fifteen light-days from Eps Eri, it had taken Creasey four daycycles to locate it. Under oath, he claimed that none aboard had survived the interval: fire, hypothermia, and anoxia had beaten him to it. (And if I wonder at what he might have hinted, with those two words, "near enough", it does no good to dwell. That way leads only to despair, faced with a question that Creasey alone could answer, and will not. And despair will not bring anyone back.)

Creasey made his choice. He opted for cover-up, secure in the knowledge that only three observatories in Eps Eri's system were sufficiently sensitive to detect the *Bougainvillaea*'s brief, feeble radio signal. And at the appointed time, thirteen daycycles after *Torosaurus* had itself detected the signal in interstellar space, and eleven daycycles after *Torosaurus* had found the *Bougainvillaea*, he finally reported the signal, initiating a fruitless search for a vessel which, by his own hand, no longer existed.

Notocero is finished, now, its board of directors placed under arrest (and, in some jurisdictions, facing execution or indefinite cryo). Documents uncovered in the ensuing investigation include a crucial memo, dated to two daycycles after the *Bougainvillaea*'s departure from Tau Ceti, and recommending that a suggestion of accidental disaster – a random and unprecedented collision with some small chunk of exotic matter, in altspace – would probably be "best to hope for in circs".

Borken, too, which was spooked by the tragedy into privately accepting that its engineering must have been responsible for the flight's loss – hence Wlodek's baroque plan to commandeer an altspace-capable vessel and flee the system before the truth came out – is on a freefall into commercial failure. All across human space, societies are debating the wisdom of altspace travel. The *Bougainvillaea*'s demise, and the manner in which it came about, has shaken humanity's confidence.

This, these secondary effects, these consequences – the fate of Borken, or of Notocero, or indeed of Creasey – they don't matter. Ultimately, nothing else matters. Only life, and loved ones, and loss. But you cannot convince some people of that.

epilogue

Has Ashé changed, in twenty years? Some. Not enough. I don't believe
it will ever change *enough*, not in my lifetime. But for now, my contract
with Borken summarily terminated, Ashé is where I am, where I'm
stuck. It's not the ending I'd have chosen for myself, but it's… alright.
It has allowed me – forced me – to reestablish contact with people I'd
left behind: Miguel, Toyah, and others. And if none of them, not even
Miguel, has dared yet to get close in any real sense, this too is alright,
and is something I understand. They keep their distance, because I'm
toxic. Foreign. Heathen. *Wrong*. And I accept that. For now.

I still have K@rine for company, at least. Not as the wooden
android, which physically remains the property of Borken, but as
the mind within, privy to so much of my history, so many of my
vulnerabilities. K@rine is, for now, a disembodied voice embedded
in my dwelling's control system – android platforms on Ashé are
expensive, and difficult to source – but her appearance was never
anything important to me. What mattered was the intellect, the trust.

I had the opportunity, had I wished, to locate myself back in
Medina, but there are too many ghosts there for me now, some of
them still warm. Instead, I've made my home in Anjanadri, a broad,
hollow-hearted monolith arcology sculpted from a hilltop in the
Acolyte Range, some twenty-five hundred kilometres due west from the

town of my birth. It's… unusual, living above ground, here on Ashé. I can see the sky, should I wish; I can see the fields of engineered crops, slowly edging their way into the boundaries of the painted desert at the mountains' feet; and, sometimes, I can see the sea, shining, some forty kilometres south. Though the terrain is different, and also the climate, there is nonetheless a familiarity to it, a recognisability. My bones tell me I am home. My mind tells me otherwise. My heart – well, which of us truly knows our own heart?

Certainly not a woman who keeps, *in memoriam*, a vase of dead flowers on her desk.

I can work from my dwelling – my apprenticeship in interstellar freighting has led to a succession of deskwork contracts – so I don't get out much. But I'm slowly beginning to mingle. I introduce myself to people, whenever I get the chance, as "the godless sexual deviant who solved the *Bougainvillaea*'s disappearance". And I revel in their discomfort, as they struggle to reconcile the fact of me, my history, with their prejudices. Will my actions help bring about change in Ashé's society? Probably not, in anything but the most minor sense.

But – and K@rine, I think, would here approve – at least I'm doing *something*.

Small presses depend on word of mouth.

If you've enjoyed this book, please mention it to friends.
Or leave a review on Goodreads, Amazon, LibraryThing, or elsewhere.

acknowledgements

I'm indebted to Thoraiya Dyer, Ian McHugh, and Rob Porteous for their constructive criticism on an earlier draft of *Flight 404*, and to Sue Bursztynski for proofreading above and beyond the call of duty.

I'm profoundly grateful to 'Looey' (Lewis P Morley) for once again providing a stunning cover image.

I'm also deeply thankful for the editorial interventions of Edwina Harvey, which have, as always, improved the telling.

Any defects that remain in the text – and there are bound to be some, for this isn't an ideal universe – are, of course, my own responsibility.

about the author

Born and raised in North Canterbury, New Zealand, Simon Petrie now lives in Canberra, Australia, with his books, his occasional ongoing forays into scientific research, and his least-effort plans for galactic domination. His short fiction has appeared in numerous places; much of it has been conveniently corralled into two now inconveniently out-of-print short fiction collections *Rare Unsigned Copy* and *Difficult Second Album*. He has been shortlisted several times for the Sir Julius Vogel, Ditmar, and Aurealis Awards, and he has won the Sir Julius Vogel Award three times: in 2010 for Best New Talent and in 2013 and 2018, with *Flight 404* and *Matters Arising from the Identification of the Body* respectively, for Best Novella. He also scored a coveted Dishonourable Mention in the 2011 Bulwer-Lytton Fiction Contest.

He has edited five issues (numbers 35, 40, 51, 54, and ~~bingo~~ 61) of *Andromeda Spaceways Inflight Magazine*, and has co-edited two anthologies (*Light Touch Paper, Stand Clear* and *Use Only As Directed*, published by Peggy Bright Books) with Edwina Harvey and one (*Next*, published by CSFG Publishing) with Rob Porteous. He's also acted as a typesetter and e-book formatter for several small-press and indie publishers in Australia and North America. He is currently a member of the Canberra Speculative Fiction Guild and SpecFicNZ writers' communities.

also by simon petrie

She took her helmet off.
That's where it starts; that's where it ends.
That's all there is.

Tanja Morgenstein, daughter of a wealthy industrialist and a geochemist, is dead from exposure to Titan's lethal, chilled atmosphere, and Guerline Scarfe must determine why.

This novella blends hard-SF extrapolation with elements of contemporary crime fiction, to envisage a future human society in a hostile environment, in which a young woman's worst enemies may be those around her.

Matters Arising from the Identification of the Body is a Sir Julius Vogel Award winning SF / mystery novella, out now.

also by simon petrie

Light levels are low. It's killingly cold. These conditions are, it transpires, connected.

The icy landscape around you—hillocks, boulders, ravines, foregrounding a hazy, rumpled horizon beneath an opaque, lowering sky—wears a patina that shades from sepia to umber, puddled with drifts of dark sand. The atmosphere, though thick, would permit only a parody of respiration: there is no succour in it. Were it not for the insulating, carefully-regulated containment of your suit, you would be dead within minutes, frozen solid within an hour.

Welcome to Titan.

Wide Brown Land: stories of Titan, out now, is a collection of eleven hard-SF short stories set on the same Titan that Guerline Scarfe calls home.

also by simon petrie

Gordon Mamon was the lift operator in a hotel that didn't have a lift.
The hotel, the 'Skyward Suites 270', was the lift.

All Gordon wants to do, when he isn't delivering room service, administering first aid, washing dishes, cleaning bathrooms, or forwarding service complaints, is to be able to finish his crossword in piece. But people keep inconsiderately dying of unnatural causes during their stay aboard his lift-module on the Skyward space elevator.

Welcome to Module 270, an orbit-transiting hotel with a suspiciously high body count.

Murder on the Zenith Express: the Gordon Mamon collection, out in October 2018, is a collection of six not-completely-serious SF mysteries.

also by simon petrie

Amorous space squids. Sentient fridges. A derelict alien spacecraft adrift within an interstellar cloud. Speed-dating zombies. The truth behind the extinction of the dinosaurs. A potentially lethal interasteroidal freight consignment. And a planet on which biological diversification has utterly failed to take hold in eight billion years.

80,000 Totally Secure Passwords That No Hacker Would Ever Guess, out in October 2018, is a misleadingly-named collection of SF short fiction, sometimes humorous and sometimes deadly serious. While several of these stories have previously appeared in the earlier collections *Rare Unsigned Copy* and *Difficult Second Album* (both now out-of-print), this new collection also includes a significant amount of newer fiction.